footprints of a living Legend

by David R. Enlow

The Story of Sam and Marie Vinton

FOOTPRINTS OF A
LIVING LEGEND

Printed in the United States of America

Contents

Chapter	Title	Page
1	Of Whom I Am Chief	1
2	The Snakes Come Out	5
3	Samarie: Living Legend	10
4	Hospitable Helpmeet	20
5	Zaire's One Great Hope	28
6	Safari, So Good	37
7	Riots, Rebellions and Roads	52
8	Oasis in the Jungle	61
9	Medicine: Open Door to the Heart	69
10	Life in the Leper Settlement	77
11	Preaching by the Printed Page	85
12	Education in Kama	93
13	They Help Hold the Fort	102
14	Days of Rebellion	107
15	Leave Your Footprints	115

I

Foreword

I met the Rev. and Mrs. Samuel R. Vinton, Sr. for the first time in 1954 at their home in what was then the Belgian Congo (now Zaire) Africa.

Almost immediately I was struck by their enthusiasm and their commitment to the ministry to which the Lord had called them in 1928. In spite of many hardships, they had carved a mission station out of the jungle which was beautiful beyond description.

All around them was the evidence of the blessing of the Lord on their ministries. Hundreds of nationals had made decisions for Christ, churches had been established, schools opened and an expanding medical work was being carried on.

Since that time I have had the privilege of returning to the Kama mission station many times. Even though the Vintons found it necessary to leave the station three times briefly during the 1960's due to political rebellions, they have continued to expand the ministries with undiminished enthusiasm.

This book tells the thrilling story of what God can accomplish through the lives of two people who have been faithful to the call of the Lord for more than 50 years. It is my prayer that many who read this book will be challenged, as the Vintons have been, to a life of service for the Lord.

Henry J. Sonneveldt
President Emeritus
Grace Mission, Inc.

Introduction

One thing should be made clear at the outset. Many stories could be told about the work of Grace Mission in Zaire, all of them exciting and challenging.

But if the story of pioneer missionaries Sam and Marie Vinton is to be told, this book must concentrate primarily on them and their ministry. Otherwise, several volumes would be required to tell the story. That necessarily means that much good work and many fine people must be omitted in the telling.

My hope and prayer is that these people will understand the limitations of the writer, and simply join the writer and other readers in thanksgiving to God for these two missionaries who have dedicated their lives to Him so faithfully.

One inevitable dilemma faced by a Christian biographer is this: How do you bring glory to God alone for His accomplishments in and through His servants? Well, hundreds of Africans and at least scores of Americans have prayed that the writer might be successful in doing that very thing. Any degree of success is due to their prayers.

How do the Vintons feel about all of this? As Sam Vinton said to me during one of our interviews at the Kama mission station, "Whenever the people out here begin to praise me for what we have been able to do, I say to them, 'God sent us; thank Him.' " And that obviously is the way that both Sam and Marie Vinton feel about their work for the Lord in Zaire.

Many friends call the Vintons "Samarie"—and aptly so, for they work together as a team. It is in that light—their oneness—that we call them a "living legend." And to tens of thousands of Africans, that is exactly what they are.

And not to the Africans alone. Lora Lee Spurlock, the energetic, dedicated wife of Wings of Calvary pilot Jack Spurlock—with whom we flew from Kama to Bukavu to Nairobi enroute home—employed the phrase "greater than Schweitzer" in her description of the Vintons.

III

A colleague and co-laborer, missionary Dr. Richard Nymeyer, is chiefly responsible for the title of this book, for in his conversation with me about the work of the Vintons, he used the words "living legend."

I am especially indebted to Henry Sonneveldt, president emeritus of Grace Mission, Inc., who accompanied me to Zaire so that I might complete research and interviews for the book. Without his help and encouragement, this project would never have been completed.

Many others have furnished helpful information. They include: Len Anderson, Charles F. Baker, Herb Birchenough, John H. Brooks, Dan Bultema, Bill and Mary Bunch, Chris V. Egemeier, Betty Frier, Martha Vinton Gardner, Ernest Green, Mrs. Lee (Pat) Green, Robert W. Harms, Helen Hoffman, E. P. Pickett, Wylma Sparks, Becky Vinton, Bill Vinton, Fred Vinton, Sam Vinton, Jr., and Theodore B. Wallin.

Sam and Marie Vinton are affectionately known to many thousands of Africans as Baba and Mama Vi *(vee).* Hundreds of times I heard those terms of endearment applied to them by grateful nationals.

Churches in Africa are gaining 15,500 new members per day, according to a global survey by Dr. David Barrett of Nairobi, Kenya. Playing a vital part in that astounding growth is the dedicated ministry of Sam and Marie Vinton.

Today the Vintons might well echo the stirring words of another missionary pioneer, David Livingston:

"People talk of the sacrifice I have made in spending so much of my life in Africa.

"Can that be called a sacrifice which is simply paid back as a part of a great debt owing to our God, which we can never repay?

"Is that a sacrifice which brings its own best reward in healthful activity, the consciousness of doing good, peace of mind, and a bright hope of a glorious destiny hereafter?

"Away with the word in that view, and with such a thought. It is emphatically no sacrifice. Say rather, it is a privilege.

"Anxiety, sickness, suffering, or danger, now and then, with a foregoing of the common conveniences and the charities of this life, may make us pause, and cause the spirit to waver and the soul to sink, but let this only be for a moment. All these are nothing when compared with the glory which shall hereafter be revealed in and for us.

"I never made a sacrifice. Of this we ought not to talk when we remember the great sacrifice He made, who left His Father's throne on high to give Himself for us."

It is safe to say that the Grace Mission board members and staff, and this author all have a common goal for this book: to honor God, to commend His faithful servants, and to challenge young people to respond to the great needs still existing today in Zaire. If that is accomplished, all our combined efforts will be richly rewarded.

—David R. Enlow

CHAPTER 1

Of Whom I Am Chief

Resplendent in his colorful tribal regalia, Chief Moligi—at his village stronghold on Kalole Hill—glared sternly at 35 of his subchiefs. He had summoned them on an urgent matter.

"You must make a choice," he began slowly, wanting to be sure no one mistook his message. "If you accept this preacher from Kama, you will no longer be headman of your village."

While his underlings shifted uneasily, Chief Moligi continued to press home his point. He had heard all he wanted to hear—and more—about Baba Vi and Mama Vi *(vee)*, African terms of endearment for Sam and Marie Vinton.

More than 50 years earlier, the American missionaries had come to Zaire with an unshakable faith in God—undeterred by years of rebellion and uprising that threatened their lives on more than one occasion. Now they faced an enemy for whom they had prayed many years.

Preferring their positions of honor to an uncertain allegiance, the majority of subchiefs responded affirmatively to their Chief's command. A few, thoroughly converted to faith in Jesus Christ, refused to obey. True to his promise, Chief Moligi stripped them of their leadership roles. That alone, however, did not satisfy the arrogant chief.

A few days later, he began a coldly calculated persecution of every Christian he confronted. In one village, he ordered the pastor to get down on his hands and knees.

"You're no better than an animal," he said. "Now eat this grass."

A man of medium height, but sturdily built, Chief Moligi gave the appearance of a professional wrestler. Immensely strong, he had lived through many years of debauchery which would have killed lesser men. Vengeance, no doubt fostered by evil spirits, led him to his stubborn coldness to the Word and its messengers.

"Christianity will make weaklings of my men," he said. "They would have to give up drinking, smoking and sexual freedom." The chief boasted of having 40 wives and innumerable children.

1

"I'll never listen to the missionaries' teaching," he promised. "I'm a rock. I can take a machete and beat upon it, and the machete will be ruined. I'm the real teacher in our villages—a teacher of drinking, polygamy and our old traditions.

"Don't ever give in," he told his subchiefs. "Their teaching is false and will come to an end; mine will endure."

With that, Chief Moligi stood up—then quietly departed as his confused leaders weighed his words carefully. Their decision would not be easy.

In subsequent weeks and months, the chief imprisoned several national preachers. Others were made to dig toilets.

Upon arrival in one village, Chief Moligi summoned all the Christians. Each was fined the equivalent of two months' wages. An elder in the Nyalukungu church, Abrahamu, and wife Sarah suffered imprisonment for a month after refusing to join a secret sect.

As the persecution continued, word came back to missionaries Sam and Marie Vinton at the Kama station, often with suggestions for countermeasures against the determined chief.

"We won't win by fighting him," Sam reminded the national believers. "That's the arm of the flesh. 'Love your enemies. Do good to them which persecute you and despitefully use you.' Let's pray for Chief Moligi."

Meanwhile, the relentless chief continued his opposition. All the members of the Mamboleo church, about 20 miles from the Kama mission station, were imprisoned for two months and fined heavily. Believers at Pene Mukunza endured the same ordeal.

His hatred growing in intensity, Chief Moligi encouraged his subchiefs to kill every preacher. His henchmen awakened the imprisoned church elders every morning at 5 o'clock to inflict 12 lashes with hippopotamus hide whips.

For 40 years, Chief Moligi fought the missionaries, national pastors and their "religion." All during this time, Marie Vinton faithfully prayed for him, especially that he would see the light of Christ—four decades of persistent, unwavering intercession.

Still unable to shake the true believers, the chief sought to force them to smoke and to drink beer—without success. When the Vintons opened a mission station in Kakumbu, unexpectedly Moligi agreed to the erection of schools and a medical center, but no Christians would be admitted, he decreed.

The chief became seriously ill a short time later. Without hesitation, Sam and Marie Vinton took special care of him in the makeshift hospital at Kama. While recovering at home and still in a weakened condition, Moligi received several personal visits from the Vintons.

"Shall we pray for you?" they asked the chief.

2

Reluctantly, the weakened leader assented—not that he really expected anything to happen, but grudging appreciation dictated his response.

"Oh, God," a compassionate Sam Vinton began, "You love this man, Chief Moligi. In fact, You loved him enough to send Your only Son, Jesus Christ, to die for him on a cross. Help him to see and understand and receive Your great love."

Unable to fathom the kind of love that met persecution with warmth and sympathy, the chief's armor began to crack—slowly but perceptibly. Soon the tears began to flow down his cheeks.

Explaining God's simple plan of salvation, the Vintons opened the door for a decision. Responding in the only way he knew how, Chief Moligi said, "I want to put my hand in God's hand!" His face seemed to glow with joy and peace, in sharp contrast to the hatred and bitterness that had been both seen and felt.

"I won't accept the Lord publicly now," he said, choosing his words carefully. "The next time you come out, I'll have all my subchiefs present and I want them to hear what I have to say."

Breathing a prayer of gratitude to God, Sam and Marie expressed their delight to the chief as they shook his hand and departed. God had rewarded four decades of fervent prayer and sowing the seed of the Word. They heard later that Chief Moligi's wives, counselors and chiefs tried to convince him to give up his faith in God. The great chief told them, "I have said what I have said. I have put my hand in God's hand."

Almost a month later, a weekend safari brought the Vintons again to Kalole Hill. True to his word, Chief Moligi summoned all 35 of his subchiefs for the occasion. Speaking before a packed audience in the village church, the transformed leader astounded his listeners.

"You know how I have fought the religion of Baba and Mama Vi," he began, great beads of perspiration glistening on his face. "I have persecuted them and the other Christians. Now I want you to know that I, too, am a Christian. Three weeks ago in my home, with Baba and Mama Vi, I received Jesus Christ into my heart and life."

Unbelieving murmurs sounded through the church, gradually changing to joyful amens and rhythmic clapping in the African tradition, as the chief continued. Amazed nationals could hardly believe their ears.

"You subchiefs," Moligi said, pointing to his 35 village leaders, "you know how I have done you wrong, how I have fought against your following God. Now I want to open the way for all of you to believe and receive this God."

Joining scores of others who responded to the Gospel invitation at the close of the service, 17 subchiefs indicated their desire and intention to receive Christ as Saviour.

3

Again, the long view—strongly recommended by Sam and Marie Vinton in considering mission accomplishments—had paid dividends, as it has on countless occasions. Their years of prayer and sowing the seed had not gone unrewarded. Not only village chiefs but also powerful witch doctors have encountered the living Christ in their performance of their duties, thanks to faithful missionaries like the Vintons.

CHAPTER 2

The Snakes Come Out

"Chief Kasongo," began the head witch doctor, Benehoka, "you must go to a healer to get rid of the snakes in your stomach. But before you do that, you should bring me a male goat."

After the chief brought a prized animal to the witch doctor, there followed three days of rituals—singing, dancing, incantations, drumming—all designed by the healer to assure him of healing in his stomach. But the cure seemed less than effective.

"I still have the snakes," Kasongo complained.

After repeating the rituals for a week, he continued to suffer.

Puzzled by the situation a young witch doctor trainee, Mali, went to see Sam Vinton at the Kama station. He knew the veteran missionary would share his usual wise counsel, mixing wisdom with compassion.

"Is our practice wrong?" the young would-be witch doctor asked.

Responding to the earnest question, Vinton explained the dangers of the procedure. Primarily, one might face painful encounters with evil spirits, always present in the jungle villages of Zaire.

Meanwhile, the distraught son of Chief Kasongo came to see the Kama missionaries also, intent on finding some solution to his father's ailment.

"Baba and Mama Vi," he began, "my father is going to die. Our healer has gone through all his magic and the snakes still haven't come out. Don't you have something that could help my father?"

"Yes," the Vintons replied, choosing their words carefully, "we think we do. Bring him in."

Three days later, Chief Kasongo came in with his son. After taking specimens, Sam Vinton treated him for ascaris (worms). The hopeful father and son went back to their home village. Four hours later, the chief returned to the Kama dispensary.

"The snakes are coming out," he reported joyfully. Eventually, Vinton counted the 117 expelled worms and saved them in a jar with formaldehyde to show the dubious witch doctor. Healing followed quickly for the grateful chief.

Unable to comprehend what had taken place, Paul Mali returned to consult with Sam Vinton. He wanted an explanation for the seeming miracle. First, the veteran missionary showed him the jar containing the "snakes" that had plagued the chief.

"Please tell me more about this," the young would-be witch doctor asked. "I need to know how to handle this kind of situation."

"Well," Vinton began, "in a way, the chief was right. He did have 'snakes' in his stomach. But your healer couldn't get them out; your witch doctor was powerless."

Mali's expression showed increasing concern. "Tell me more," he begged. "You once mentioned something about God."

Pausing for careful and prayerful thought before he spoke, Sam Vinton offered an explanation.

"You see," he said, "I am talking about the living God, about His Son, Jesus Christ, who gave His life for us. In God's sight we are all sinners, in need of a Saviour."

Mali interrupted, a puzzled frown still creasing his brow, "What is sin?" he asked with obvious sincerity.

"Well," Vinton suggested, warming to the question, "sin is anything that displeases God. And the god your witch doctor and your healer are talking about isn't the same God we are talking about."

Wanting to digest what he had heard thus far, the young man thanked the missionary, excused himself and returned to his village. He must tell his superior what he had learned.

After relating his conversation with Vinton, young Paul Mali added: "And Baba Vi says God doesn't get angry at us; He loves us. He hates sin, but He loves sinners."

Though warned to cease his search for truth, Mali returned to ask more questions of his spiritual mentor. Patiently, lovingly, the wiry, deeply tanned missionary explained again God's plan of salvation. Now Mali knew he was ready; he must not delay. "I want to be a child of God," he said.

Sam Vinton proceeded without hesitation. "The Bible says, 'As many as received Him (the Lord Jesus Christ) to them gave He the power to become sons (children) of God.' Are you ready and willing to receive Him right now?"

Paul Mali waited no longer; his questions had been answered; his heart had been satisfied. Great joy came to his heart as he voiced an eternal yes to God, indicating a deliberate choice to serve and follow Him.

Returning to his family and to his superior, the erstwhile witch doctor explained what had taken place. Indignantly, one by one, they ostracized him, inviting him to leave and never return. Heartbroken, the torn young man faced the decision of a lifetime.

6

'I'm going to follow the God of Baba and Mama Vi," he proclaimed as he departed from his village, uncertain of his future but determined to stick by his commitment.

Coming back to Kama, the young convert received a warm welcome. Vinton had engaged a number of young men to saw lumber, part of an expanding building program he had instituted in the village. Now he placed Paul Mali in charge of the crew, and the jubilant youth responded faithfully and effectively.

Later, when young Mali met the girl of his choice and wanted to marry her, his family would not provide the necessary dowry. The Vintons took care of that need, and the wedding proceeded. That began a long and fruitful life of service for the Lord.

Today, the Paul Malis have two sons, Paul Jr. and Peter. The older son, Paul, pastors one of the churches in a village some 45 miles from Kama, while Peter is in a commercial business in a village 150 miles away. Both are outstanding Christians, singers and active for the Lord.

Again, God had reached into the heart and life of a confused man—this time a would-be witch doctor; earlier a village chief. And other nationals from all walks of life responded to the Gospel message as well. Followers of Mohammed were not excluded from the effective witness of the Vintons.

"I am a Mukusu," declared Kilubi Armazani, recounting his earlier days. "My father died when I was very small and my uncle who raised me was a follower of Islam. So I was brought up in that religion, but it didn't bring anything into my heart.

"As a young man I left home and went to Kindu. There I entered the Catholic school and followed that religion. I got a lot of things into my head but not a thing into my heart."

After two years, Armazani recalled, he left school and got a job in a store. The white man gave him merchandise and sent him out to sell the goods in far-away villages, so he became a traveling salesman—going along with several porters who carried the merchandise.

"During that time," he continued, "I married wives and I cast off wives. I followed in all the ways of sin . . . living for myself. I liked to drink, too. When my heart would condemn me for my bad ways, I always excused myself that everyone else was doing the same thing."

Pausing thoughtfully, the young man added, "I got tired of my work and became a mason, and I have been doing that work many years for the government, and then for the gold mines. My last wife and I came to a parting of the ways and I have been living alone for the past four years.

"The government moved me to Imonga this past year. It is a large camp with more than 200 workmen plus their families. Three

7

religions are followed—Islam, Catholic and Protestant. I didn't attend service anywhere but just looked on."

Kilubi Armazani hesitated a moment before proceeding. "In my heart there was a hunger for something, I didn't know what. I started going to the Protestant teacher's house to ask him questions about things on my heart. He was very patient with me and taught me many things I had never heard before in my life. He was always reading to me from the New Testament. My heart kept on being hungry, but that was all the further I got.

"Then on April 27, Baba and Mama Vinton came to hold meetings at Imonga and I went over to the chapel. Well, something happened to me! I just gave myself over to the Lord. I felt like all my burdens had rolled off my back. I received the Lord Jesus Christ into my heart (not my head) and I am now His child."

Armazani wanted to be sure he was heard across the water. "Christians in America, I want you to remember me in your prayers, because I am just a newborn babe in Christ. My fellow workmen jeer and insult me, but I want to live and be a light for Him in this place of darkness. Pray that I may grow and be strong in the Lord."

At the Kama mission station Sam and Marie Vinton continue a spiritual and physical witness on a daily basis—part of a lifelong commitment to this adopted country. From many miles around, men and women, boys and girls, and babies come to the dispensary for treatment. Many others come to the hospital in more serious cases. If the need arises outside of regular "office" hours, the patients simply walk across the compound to the Vinton residence and wait outside to be recognized.

Sometimes they can't wait. An emergency sends them rushing for help, and they make their need known as soon as they arrive.

"Hodi! Hodi!" That shrill cry reached Sam and Marie one day as they sat down for lunch. Walking to the door, they saw a familiar sight—a frightened African mother with her infant in arms. She had walked *four days* to seek medical assistance.

"My baby is sick," she cried. "Can you help me?"

Without a moment's hesitation, the Vintons left their lunch and walked with their distraught patient across the attractive station grounds to the dispensary, perhaps a hundred yards away. Gravel footpaths criss-cross the station's beautiful green lawn, and they took the quickest route to the brick clinic, briskly covering the short distance despite their seven decades of vigorous, energy-depleting service.

Administering equal doses of love and medicine, Samarie saw an expected change before their eyes. In a matter of minutes they had brought relief to the feverish child, and a grateful mother wept tears of joy. Her warm smile provided sufficient reward for the pioneer missionaries.

8

Later the same afternoon, a Zairian couple arrived carrying a desperately sick infant. They had walked sixteen miles and crossed two rivers in a dug-out canoe before alternately walking and running the final mile to the Kama mission station—truly a spiritual oasis in the jungle.

Again, the deft, capable hands of the missionary couple, always sensitive to the total needs of their patients, provided relief. And jubilant parents gave heartfelt thanks for such tender care.

"Thank you, Baba Vi. Thank you, Mama Vi." Such expressions of gratitude provide all the reward the Vintons need, though a minimal charge (about ten cents) is made for service to patients.

"We never want to rob them of their dignity and self-respect," the missionaries explain. Baba Vi's philosophy is, "Nothing for nothing," and the nationals applaud his views.

Another day, Mama Vi sat on the veranda of the Vintons' brick home when a young African mother walked up the footpath just in front of the residence, holding a child by one hand and a big bag with the other. With typical courtesy, she waited for recognition.

"Do you remember me?" the beaming, though obviously tired, woman asked.

"No, I'm sorry, but I don't," Marie responded.

Bibi Mugeni explained that she had come to Kama four years earlier for infertility treatments. Her childless marriage had been threatened, since barrenness in their culture is considered sufficient cause for polygamy or divorce. Now she had come to show off her 3-year-old Clementine Maombi (meaning "prayers"), actually walking 67 miles over four days to bring rice and chicken to the Vintons in appreciation.

Fifty years of such incidents involve virtually a lifetime of miracles for the missionary couple. These pioneers came to the Belgian Congo (now Zaire) in 1928 and have taken only three short furloughs in all that time, so dedicated have they been to the Lord and the task He entrusted to them.

CHAPTER 3

'Samarie': Living Legend

"God must still need us here; He keeps renewing our strength."

That is the daily miracle of Sam and Marie Vinton—'Samarie' to many friends—who despite their advancing years (mid-70's) continued a backbreaking schedule into the 80's that would tax men and women half their age.

Baba Vi, how much of your goal have you achieved?

"By 1958," Sam Vinton explains, "I had entirely achieved our original goal locally. I discovered I had limited my goal. We must go beyond our community. We want to get out and evangelize all 306 villages in our area of responsibility.

"Our goal is ten new churches each year. Through the first ten months of 1979, 12 new churches had been established. Our present area of responsibility—with Kama as the hub—involves a radius of about 120 miles, encompassing close to half a million people."

How did you establish such a warm rapport with the nationals?

"From the very outset, we began to break down the barriers between the missionaries and the Africans. We shook hands with the nationals at every opportunity; ate with them; invited them into our home; always made them feel welcome."

On one occasion national pastor Mubule Paul was hurt. Baba Vi asked his carriers to transport the injured man. "We will carry you, but never a black man," they responded.

Disturbed but undaunted, Vinton took hold of the carrying poles that would help to support the ailing pastor. Some of the nationals—aware of the sterling example—followed his lead, and eventually did all the carrying.

What is the most unique feature of your ministry?

"Living among, working with, preaching to and teaching the same people at one place has to be a unique experience, and we are most grateful for it. God has enabled us to become involved with individuals, families, churches and communities in a greater way than ever before."

Do you have a special philosophy about the physical needs of the people?

10

"Our medical work is not based on curing-healing. Rather we work to clear away obstructions to allow God and nature to heal. At each clinic national pastors teach Scripture to the waiting patients and pray for them.

"Then we are ready to get rid of physical obstructions: anti-malarial drugs to rid the body of that killer; antibiotics to get rid of infections; worm medicines to destroy intestinal parasites; vitamins to aid the healing powers.

"Too, we have a preventive program: safe drinking water; encouraging good toilets; planting fruit trees; producing and eating good food; palm oil extraction, providing shortening for cooking needs."

How did you happen to become a missionary?

"When God picked me up and made me a missionary, it was His doing. All I did was obey. I had other plans—of all kinds. But I came out because I wanted to be obedient."

How do you account for the fact that in your 70's you are still able to carry on a tremendous load of work and responsibility?

"Well, at least two things come to mind. First, of course, is the strength that God pours in day by day. 'As thy days, so shall thy strength be.' Second, we have never let any bitterness come into our hearts, regardless of the situation."

Don't you ever have any problems?

"We are asked that many times, and my answer is always the same. Yes, we do have problems, but I don't have time to worry and talk about them. God is doing too many wonderful things to stop and concentrate on the problems."

Have you made any radical changes in the way things are done on the mission field?

"As soon as I came to Kama, I began to outlaw three things: pith helmets, daily quinine and spine packs. I really didn't see any great need for them. And when the nationals saw that the missionaries could get along without them, they became willing to break with custom and tradition."

As we talked, a sudden rumble approached and shook the house as if by a giant vibrator. Vinton answered questions about the interruption very calmly. "Just an earthquake," he replied matter-of-factly. "We have a few of them every year." Except for falling ceilings and momentary terror, little damage is done by the tremors.

Is there anything in particular Americans and others could learn from the living habits of the Africans?

"One thing comes to mind immediately, and that is the African practice of the extended family. It is a way of life for them to be taking in visitors, members of their own clan or tribe—many times

11

people on their way to the dispensary or hospital and needing a place to stop overnight."

Are there any major differences between Christian workers here and in America?

"Well, yes. In America, everybody's a specialist; in Kama, one has to be a specialist in everything."

Typical of Sam Vinton's sensitivity to nationals is his practice of giving away his well-marked Swahili New Testaments at least once a year to chiefs and other village leaders. They are always highly prized and serve a two-fold purpose: (1) an expression of love, and (2) further dissemination of the good news of the Gospel.

Many years earlier, a Methodist bishop shared with Vinton a missionary philosophy that Sam and Marie have practiced for more than five decades:

"Do not take a critical attitude. In other words, do not criticize what you find. Go out and proclaim the Gospel. Present Christ. When the old leaves drop off, then new leaves will appear. God will raise the people up to something better."

Just outside the open door leading to the Vintons' dining room is a sink and faucet, complete with germicidal soap and towel. Automatically, whenever he returns from the dispensary or the hospital, Vinton goes to the sink and washes his hands carefully. Now, as he walks to the veranda for a few minutes' rest, he sees 3-year-old Salima—cuddly, smiling and dimpled—waiting for him in his chair, her gleaming white teeth shining like pearls against the dark background. In a moment's time, she is in his lap, snuggling up to the wiry missionary and whispering childlike thoughts in his ear.

Still giving close attention to his tiny admirer, Vinton shares further aspects of his philosophy. "If you want to make a success of your work, you must know your people. Think black!"

Speaking in a clipped English accent that betrays a strong familiarity with French and Swahili, the tanned, five-foot-eleven missionary admits he often has to search for the proper English word. Fifty years with the nationals has colored his speech considerably.

When food poisoning struck the whole missionary family back in 1976, Vinton recalled, hundreds of nationals came in to pray.

"Lord," one older woman prayed fervently, "You sent these people to us. You know You can't let them die. The villagers will say, 'He's not really God if He lets them die.' They will say our God is not real."

Famed missionary physician, Dr. Carl Becker, came to the station and ministered to the ailing Americans. Though six of the missionaries almost died, God did hear and answer the prayers of His people, and they all recovered.

"Yes," Vinton said, "it was a little testing time, but God takes care of His people."

Never really alone for long at a time, Sam Vinton responds to frequent passersby as he sits on his veranda, and they always seem to leave smiling and in good spirits. Some personal problem has been shared, thus easing the burden for the bearer.

When an occasional visitor requires his attention at the dispensary, Vinton strides erectly across the compound, stopping briefly along the way to pat a black boy or girl on the head and give a word of encouragement and good cheer.

Explaining the late arrival of some patients, far beyond the clinic's 7:00 a.m. opening hour, the 73-year-old missionary calls attention to the rainy weather. "They come more by atmosphere than by the hour," he explains.

Cool Kama evenings by the fireplace in the Vinton den may seem like a dream, but reality comes quickly as a mouse scurries in the corner and flying ants pester anyone close to lights. A Delco generator provides light from 6:15 to 8:30 each evening, and the missionary residences and guest houses have fluorescent lighting available for a short while after that.

"Lord,"-Sam Vinton had prayed many years earlier, "I must have lights. You know we need electricity. I'm willing to sleep on boards, but we must have lights." The 12-volt generator provided the first lighting.

How do you feel about the indigenous principle of missions (training nationals to carry on their own work)?

"Our original call—our vision—was to go somewhere and create a Christian community, building on no other man's work. We wanted it to be complete with church, school, farm, medical center, building and carpentry. From the very beginning, our program has been to train these people to carry on their own work.

"I have men now for every phase of the work—well trained to carry on—but I have no one who is manager, coordinator, director, who can bring these things together. They have not developed far enough along.

"I have trained fellows in OB work, but they won't perform unless I am there. They believe there is a special power in my hands. My hands now are sensitive enough to feel when a spleen is infected, for example. I can detect many physical problems simply by feel. They believe in the touch of my hands."

Is your ministry aimed at any particular class of nationals?

"We have been accused at times of being missionaries to the chiefs, the commercial leaders, magistrates, hierarchy—influential people. Actually, I felt they were the neglected ones—nobody bothered about them. I have become great friends with many influential people and it has paid off.

"The number of Christian chiefs in our area today is remarkable. And the further away from the Kama station you go, the fewer Christians you find.

"The Apostle Paul visited and worked in a place, then left. True, but he worked with educated, cultured people. If Paul were here today, he would probably do what we are doing."

Do you see any specific needs in the national churches today?

"One in particular comes to mind. We need Christian laymen who are known for their honesty and integrity in business. Usually, the only white people the nationals see are missionaries and pastors, so they naturally conclude that all Christians eventually become missionaries or pastors.

"When my son, Fred, said, 'Dad, I can't be a missionary like Sam (Jr.),' I told him, 'Son, I don't want you to be like anyone else; I want you to be what the Lord wants you to be. Maybe He wants you to start a rice mill.' "

Fred Vinton followed his father's advice, and today in America his reputation still is that of one who deals squarely in business.

Can you give an example of the type of important lessons you have to teach the people?

"They make beer from palm trees. Often I tell them, 'If you drink a bottle of beer on top of my medicine, you will have a fire down in your stomach.' They seem to identify with the feeling."

How did you become a specialist in so many things?

"My Dad put me through a wonderful training school—his own. I learned agriculture; became an apprentice builder in a big lumber factory for prefab homes; earned many practical merit badges as an Eagle Scout; became captain of the first aid team in the mines of Pennsylvania.

"That experience went a long way toward enabling us to build houses out here that have stood for 45 years, and the swamp leaf roofs last for 20 years."

Why have you taken only three short furloughs during your long missionary career?

"Several factors are involved. Furloughs are intended primarily for those who need them; we have rarely felt that need. On one occasion, I worked with a man for six months who was to replace me while we went on furlough. When the time came for us to go, the man said, 'If you leave, I'll leave too.'

"One time we returned from furlough and learned that 23 nationals had died in a measles epidemic. The Africans told us it would not have happened if we had been here. That undoubtedly has colored our thinking whenever talk of furlough arises."

Did you once receive criticism for sending your children home to America alone?

"Yes. The children had never been home (to grandparents in Pennsylvania). Tad (Sam Jr.) was 13; Bud (Fred) was 11; Richie (George Richard) was 8. We kept Betty with us. We had prayed much about the decision and felt they should go.

"True to His Word, God takes care of His own. The children were scheduled to stay in Kinshasa for a week (1200 miles from Kama) before they could fly out. But an American businessman—Ralph Loper, of Falls River, Mass., who had been sent to Zaire by the American Government to check on uranium—saw them there, heard their story, and asked if they would like to fly home with him.

"Instead of having to wait for a week, they went out the very next day on the flight to New York. When the time came for them to return to Zaire, they were unable to obtain visas. Hearing of their plight, a top Zairian official sent word to the authorities: 'By order of the Governor of Kivu, give the Vinton boys visas.' "

Even while recounting past joys and victories, trials and sorrows, Vinton's active mind and observant eyes call attention to such things as the nearby garden where the missionaries grow green beans, cassava, manioc, cucumbers, tomatoes, corn, eggplant and cabbage. And as he talks, an African mother and her daughter walk up to the veranda, the older woman holding her jaw.

Excusing himself, Vinton strides briskly toward the dispensary, his patient and her daughter following at a respectful distance behind. After pulling a badly abscessed tooth, the medical missionary returns to his veranda. He begins to recall his early experiences on the field.

More than fifty years earlier, as a young man of 20, Sam Vinton felt the call to Africa. "You're too young," a mission board told him. But the call was too clear to ignore.

After Sam had talked with his father about the matter, the wise parent said, "If you want to take a trip for a year and then come back to America and finish your schooling, I'll pay your way."

Sam countered with a promise. "If I go out and see that I've made a mistake, I won't be too proud to come back home." The Lord opened the way, and the long journey began. Enroute by ship, the young man spent much of his time learning Swahili—a step that gave him a warm reception by the nationals at the very outset of his illustrious missionary career.

Forty years later, Sam Vinton—by now a household name in scores of villages and thousands of mud huts—could face an overflow anniversary celebration in the church and say to scores of chiefs and other eager listeners:

"How many hands do you have? Two? So do I. In this hand I brought the Word of God. In the other hand I brought tools—saws, syringes and so on. You cannot develop your country without both. You need the Word of God and you need to know how to work."

As he handed each chief a Bible and a machete, Vinton heard the shouts and cheers of excited nationals. They obviously agreed with his emphasis to their leaders.

In what ways have you pioneered in this work?

"For one thing, our homes are made of brick. And we have done away with window panes, substituting wire screens. We believe in fresh air.

"We are still the only mission station with weekend safaris *(kusanyikos:* "gathering in"). From seven to fifteen churches band together to hold a conference in one of the villages. The host church provides everything, except that visiting groups bring in food and firewood. They are a tremendous strengthening for the believers."

Later, Sam Vinton and his well-organized safari team would take his visitors on one of these unbelievable, yet amazingly effective journeys.

Does your ministry have a special emphasis?

"Yes, we have emphasized the abundant life in everything we do. But we have made very clear the fact that a person can't have an abundant life until he has life." Various methods are used to get that message across.

Talking drums are a normal way of communication in many villages of Zaire, particularly in the expansive Kama area. The only white man ever to be given a code name for use on the talking drums is Sam Vinton. His name is "Lukenekene" (The Star That Travels by Night).

What concrete evidence do you see today of changed lives and habits?

"Among the many things that could be named are the 223 idol worship shrines that have been torn down and replaced by houses of worship. But better than this outward, visible change is the transformation that has taken place in thousands of lives."

Vinton is a great believer in mottoes and slogans. One that characterizes his life is this: "To know God's will is the greatest secret of successful living; to do God's will is the greatest joy in life." On his Bible bookmark are these words: "I am not disobedient to the heavenly vision. I can do all things through Christ who gives me the strength. I must work; He must give me the strength."

Another Vinton favorite: "One with God is a majority." And still another: "Only he who sees the invisible can do the impossible."

Vinton is convinced that the people in the Kama area need missionaries now more than ever before—not only for direction and coordination of the work, but also for encouragement and counsel.

"I often get tired *in* the work," he admits, "but I never get tired *of* the work."

An awesome responsibility rests on the slender shoulders of the veteran missionary. As one church leader said to him recently, "Baba Vi, be careful what you say. Your words can bring life or death, good or bad, joy or sorrow."

Family, friends and co-laborers of the Vintons agree that many outstanding qualities characterize the pioneer couple.

"The people among whom they work have an overwhelming confidence in their leadership," declared Theodore B. Wallin, who first met Sam Vinton in 1931 when they studied Tropical Medicine together in Belgium. "Especially do I remember their complete trust in the Lord and their thoughtfulness for people."

Lennart Anderson, a colleague beginning in 1946, recalled: "Sam Vinton always was a great preacher. He could keep the audience on the edge of their seats for an hour." Then he recalled an example of his friend's uncommon courage.

"When I was at Kama in 1970, times were difficult and the people had not really settled down. One day one of the teachers, from the Watusi tribe, flunked some of the students in his class. The entire school was aroused. They came in the evening, armed with rocks and chains and knives to get this 'strange' teacher.

"Sam stood alone in front of the man's house and told that mob they could not pass by on the teacher's property. For an hour he stood there. At last they backed down and returned to their homes."

Charles F. Baker, president emeritus of Grace Bible College, referred to the self-sacrifice, faithfulness, hard work, love, compassion, versatility and enthusiasm of the Vintons. "They came to feel that Africa was their home, and they would not be happy anywhere else as long as they were able to minister to these people."

Chris V. Egemeier, friend and co-laborer for 30 years, recalled the Vintons' ability to laugh in the face of frustration and disappointment.

"They have exercised great skill and patience in developing workmen and potential leaders: cooks, houseboys, gardeners, carpenters, masons, clerks, church elders and pastors. Vinton-trained nationals have been in great demand by other missionaries as well as by Belgian administrators and mine officials."

A graduate of Indiana (Pa.) High School, with later study at the Pittsburgh Bible Institute, Sam Vinton had been accepted by the Evangelization Society Africa Mission in 1928 and assigned to the Belgian Congo. That was ten years before Grace Mission, current supporting body, came into existence as the Worldwide Grace Testimony Mission.

Then Vinton and missionary nurse Helen Hoffman, along with three other co-laborers, traveled from New York to Dar es Salaam to Kigoma to Albertville by train and boat. Eventually arriving at Kindu, a river port and railway terminal, they traveled nine long days on forest trails to Shabunda. Two months had elapsed since their New York departure.

A short time later, Sam accepted assignment to the Kama station, almost 100 miles south of Shabunda, in the heart of the Warega tribe territory. Replacing Mr. and Mrs. Jacob Everhard, who were returning to the States after five years of intense traveling and evangelizing, Sam later welcomed Raymond Moore and Mr. and Mrs. James Summers as colleagues.

Appalled by the physical suffering he saw on every side, Vinton knew he must include healing for the body with the spiritual. Close to 90 percent of the people suffered from yaws, dread tropical disease that produced ugly ulcers and resulted in permanent disfigurement for many.

Sam knew he could not stand by and watch 50 percent of the infants die from malaria before they reached their first birthday. (Today that figure is less than 10 percent.) He must do what he could and he prayed earnestly for direction. Earlier experience as assistant to a physician and a dentist back in Pennsylvania had given him a prayerful interest and a working knowledge of the medical field.

After completion of his tropical medicine studies in Antwerp, Belgium, along with a further study of French at the same time, Vinton decided against returning immediately to the field.

After a whirlwind ten-week tour of supporting churches in the United States, Sam went to Europe for four months of training at *L'Alliance Francaise* in Paris. A new young missionary, James Hillyard, accompanied him.

Upon arrival back in the Congo, Sam received a month of practical training at the government hospital in Albertville. That gave him official recognition as an *agent sanitaire,* the French equivalent of a male nurse. Now he felt much better qualified to give physical as well as spiritual help to the people he served.

While studying in Europe, Sam had carried on an extensive correspondence with a single lady missionary who had come out under the same board. They had met several years earlier at a Bible conference in Pennsylvania.

Her name was Marie Mikula. The two became one as they wed in Kigoma, on the other side of Lake Tanganyika from Albertville, in 1932 and arrived at their Kama station in May of that year.

If ever a couple complemented each other in the work to which God had called them, Sam and Marie Vinton comprise that couple.

Like her husband, Mama Vi has earned a warm place in the hearts of the African people. A look at highlights of her career gives ample reason for the respect she receives.

CHAPTER 4

Hospitable Helpmeet

People take priority over everything else in the lives of Sam and Marie Vinton, and that requires almost round-the-clock hospitality on the part of matronly Mama Vi, who at 74 carries her five-foot-four frame erectly as she serves coffee, tea and extras to whatever guests happen to be present at a given moment.

Usually wearing a colorful *kikwembe,* typical African women's ankle-length dress, Marie has a daily program that might stagger the imagination—not to mention the stamina—of the ordinary American housewife. True, she has some help from well-trained nationals who serve as houseboys, but even so she carries on some household duties along with a medical ministry that extends beyond what might be considered normal "office hours."

Every morning, in addition to the clinic crowds, upwards of a dozen women and children gather in back of the Vinton residence to be treated for measles or whooping cough, and they are Marie's responsibility. Many have traveled several miles to secure the treatment, and some have not had time for breakfast. A hot cup of tea or coffee with a bowl of oatmeal makes the long wait worthwhile.

Most patients receive ampicillin given orally, along with proper instructions on how to take care of themselves. Generous doses of TLC (tender, loving care) accompany each treatment, and that happy combination usually brings quick relief.

Whenever testing or trial comes her way, Mama Vi confidently affirms, "That is one of the 'all things'!" obviously referring to Romans 8:28.

At many mealtimes, Mama Vi begins by reading from *Our Daily Bread. Favorites,* by Richard W. DeHaan and Henry G. Bosch. Then a promise box verse is shared with each diner, and the others are expected to quote the correct reference. No verse ever goes unidentified, for Mama Vi seems to be a walking lexicon of Bible references.

After reading Colossians 4:5 ("Walk in wisdom toward them th

20

are without, redeeming the time") Sam Vinton interjects his own private interpretation of the verse: "If you want to kill time, work it to death."

With typical Vinton hospitality, guests—like Jack and Lora Lee Spurlock, before one of their return flights to Bukavu—receive a hearty breakfast of oatmeal, omelet, toast and tea, or coffee.

Mama Vi graciously reminds her diners of the importance of the Spurlocks to their ministry. "That plane is our lifeline," she says. "It is responsible for bringing us medicines, food and mail."

That gift for saying the right thing at the right time—a word in season—characterizes the daily life of Marie Vinton. As she plays and jokes with the three children of Richard and Jane Nymeyer (Jaylene, 11; Julie, 8; Jennifer, 5), their co-laborers on the station, Mama Vi is chided by Jane.

"You spoil our kids," the younger missionary says with obvious appreciation. "You know you can't spoil a good thing," Marie retorts without a moment's hesitation.

Sam Vinton gratefully recounts the fact that "we have never had any problem in our family over the years with dysentery or diarrhea, because Mama Vi always takes care of our water and fresh vegetables to see that they are protected. She uses a timer to adhere rigidly to a 20-minute boiling time for all drinking and cooking water."

When sleepiness or sickness interferes with her routine, Marie is a study in selflessness. While Sunday evening devotions among the missionaries and guests proceed, she sits quietly with eyes closed—sometimes praying, often catching a few much-needed winks.

One day Jane Nymeyer saw Marie in a chair almost asleep, but obviously suffering. Helping her to bed and administering chloroquin, Jane thus minimized a two-week bout with malaria for the older woman. But never a word of complaint from Mama Vi or even a mention of her physical ailments.

If learning to adapt and adjust is the hallmark of successful missionaries, then Sam and Marie Vinton eminently qualify for that characterization of their work. Without a refrigerator for the first 19 years of their service in Kama, they learned how to prepare meals—one by one, day after day—off the land. Because limeade kept best in the heat, they drank a lot of the tasty beverage from the fruit right off their own trees.

Visitors in the guest house learn to expect a warm, salutatory, handwritten memo from Mama Vi each morning, delivered by the quiet, courteous houseboy. "Good morning—a light heart and a bright day. Breakfast at our house—7:50. DV.—MV" Or, "VIPs . . . . Good morning! I have been trying to jog over . . . but . . . please give Malumba your bath towels to get sunned. BCNU. P.S. Send laundry, too!" Or, "Good morning! Serving pre-breakfast coffee and tea at the fireplace now—any time! And breakfast will be at 7:00 while waiting for the sun to come out to dry out the road."

When a widow dropped by with a gift and a word of appreciation for Mama Vi, she explained the background. "When a man dies it is the custom for his family to take everything that belonged to the couple before his death. This widow has TB and gets her medicine here; she has nowhere else to turn. Now she has come just to express her thanks, not only to us but also indirectly to Edna Mae Egemeier, who sent her a dress recently."

Not many minutes pass before an African girl approaches the veranda. She, too, has TB and is returning one of the medicine bottles for a refill. In typical extended-family fashion, she is staying in the nearby village after a walk of many miles. Not many yards away, Baba Vi can be seen walking regally from the hospital to the dispensary. He and Marie exchange waves as he passes within thirty yards of the Vinton home.

When Sam and Marie came home from Africa on April 20, 1963, it marked their first furlough in 35 years. After brief visits to family and friends, they traveled to several states in the East and Midwest sharing highlights of their ministry on the Dark Continent. Typically, Sam and Marie spent only about three months away from their home in the Congo.

Before their return to the field, Mama Vi underwent an operation for removal of the thyroid gland. "At the Grace Gospel Fellowship convention in July," she wrote later, "several ladies asked me the name of the hospital so they could write me. Well, what a surprise! I received more than one hundred cards, which was overwhelming, I assure you."

With a real gift for communication, Marie often shares mission highlights with readers of *Outreach,* published by their supporting Grace Mission in Grand Rapids, Michigan.

"I was aroused out of a deep sleep," she began in one such communique. "It was three o'clock. I listened for some sound, wondering what had awakened me—but not a sound was to be heard.

"Our 'Mr. Owl' was off somewhere; the hyrax (a little nocturnal animal that lives in the tall trees) was off elsewhere crying about his 'lost tail'; and the frogs at the stream behind us were strangely silent."

Marie lay awake wondering about the unusual stillness. Then, suddenly, there came over the hill—she just could not believe it—the sound of *singing!*

"Listening, I heard, 'In tenderness He sought me, weary and sick with sin . . . Oh, the love that sought me . . . ' In Swahili, of course. All five verses were sung. Not just a few but many voices sang with wonderful assurance. Sometimes I sang along with them, and again just listened with heart overflowing with praise.

"A short silence, then over the hill came the voices again with another song. Truly, it was 'songs in the night.' My heart rejoiced with the singers and sent up a big 'thank You, Lord' for this precious experience."

Instead of the beating of drums, pagan incantations to drive off the evil spirits, Mama Vi recalled, here was a clear witness to everyone in the chief's village that night.

"My husband, Sam, had taken the school inspector back to Bukavu. I regretted that he was not here to share this wonderful experience.

"The previous morning, family members thought the wife of the village blacksmith had died. Later, however, they discovered a very faint pulse so rushed to the Mission for medical help. The patient was given a heart stimulant and other medicine, and had lingered on throughout the day and into the night."

Now, Marie remembered, the Christian relatives of the woman who were keeping vigil over her were bearing her up with songs of praise to God.

"In the morning," Mama Vi continued, "we sent a huge kettle of tea for the family and special food for the patient. She continued to convalesce and later was able to get to the government hospital 85 miles away for further treatment and surgery.

"Amisi, the blacksmith, told me how his father-in-law had been touched during the time of his daughter's illness. 'You know,' he said, 'you Christians have something—an *assurance*—that my religion does not give me. I would like to have it. I am going to attend church at the village chapel and hear for myself.'

"May 'songs in the night' continue in this land as a testimony for our Lord," Marie concluded.

One of her co-laborers in the '50's, Wylma Sparks, recalled some of Mama Vi's unusual traits. "The rainy season started, and it seemed as though it would rain forever—one of the worst they had ever experienced. Mama Vi decided to cover the cushions on the porch, not quite so frivolous a project as it seemed since many meetings were held on the Vintons' front porch.

"We had a shopping center nearby, but supplies were limited since Independence. The only yard goods available were solid bright green and orange, no prints. Mama Vi, undaunted, sewed a triangle of orange to a triangle of green, making a square for the cushion."

She ended up with a bright, cheery-looking porch, Wylma recalls. Marie met every problem she encountered with the same common-sense approach. Her friends rarely saw her flustered or upset—a result of a lifetime spent in coping with the unexpected on a daily, sometimes hourly, basis.

"Her favorite verse," Wylma continued, "seemed to be Ephesians 3:20, 'Now unto Him that is able to do exceeding abundantly above all that we ask or think . . . .' She looked on all of life's little extras as an 'abundantly above.' Her favorite expression in prayer was, 'Lord, we are a needy people.'

"I never saw her discouraged—a result, I believe, of a lifetime spent living by faith in God's ability, not her own."

In still another colorful, descriptive report to her supporters and readers, Marie Vinton revealed something of the great variety of work in which she was engaged:

"This is rice harvest time in all of the Kama area. The men felled and burned the trees, cleared the fields in July and August. The women planted in September and now in March they are in the fields early in the morning until late afternoon cutting the sheaves and carrying the huge baskets on their backs into their villages.

"The fields are from two to five miles in distance, so that isn't just a little 'promenade.' "

For the past few weeks, Mama Vi recalled, each Sunday the women came in with their "first offering" unto the Lord. The bowls and basins contained from two to ten pounds or more.

"Most of the families will not have their first meal of new rice until they have brought this 'thank offering' to the Lord," Marie continued.

"We have a women's meeting every Friday at four . . . . The offerings are going to be used to buy palm oil for the women at the leper settlement . . . . Some have been there for many years and cast off by their husbands . . . . There are some precious Christians among them."

They planned to go out with a group (only four miles) and take the oil to them, one bottle for each woman . . . . How they appreciated the bandages that were sent!

"Our days are filled with little 'inasmuch' tasks—young mothers with nursing problems, crying hungry babies, sick children, maternity patients and any special patients needing extra food," Marie added.

"Six-year-old Adela was brought in looking like a skeleton. She had begun with measles and followed with chest complications. After six weeks she was able to go back home, well again and able to sing. Her father is a great song leader and she likes to sing, too."

Mama Vi then remembered that "the other day another five-year-old was brought in, crying pitifully with boils. Sam is treating her and we are feeding her and encouraging her mother to trust the Lord for her child.

"I had a nice surprise this week. A young mother walked 15 miles to see us. She greeted me with, 'Here is your preemie. He brought you a bottle of fresh peanut oil.' I thanked 'preemie' for the oil and just praised the Lord for this beautiful baby.

"We have classes for the grade school girls three mornings each week. We are still 'sowing and sewing.' We do need your prayers for these girls."

The high school girls asked for a special class for them, Marie recalled, so they had been meeting for the past month on the Vinton porch, every Saturday afternoon. They made quilt square bags for their crochet work. Then they had good discussions over tea and pancakes.

"These girls are a terrific challenge, with a wonderful opportunity of planting and harvesting His Word in their hearts," Marie concluded.

Another former colleague of the Vintons, William D. Bunch, singled out the "stick-to-itiveness, love, compassion, concern, desire to help these people help themselves, the idea of 'nothing for nothing' " as traits that impressed him during his work with them.

Bunch cited as among their outstanding accomplishments "the establishing of 229 churches with more than 15,000 members; the organization of a vast network of elementary schools; building bridges; establishing mission stations at Kama and Kakumbu.

"Problems of sickness, disease, certain tribal customs caused the deaths of many children," Bunch recalled. "These were solved by the Vintons' vision of mobile clinics, of going out to the people rather than having most of them coming in to him."

Rebellions, mutinies, all of these things were overcome by their ability to rebound in spite of difficulties and never giving up, Bunch remembered. Lack of food, lack of communication, constant problems were caused by the upheavals.

"In 1960," Bunch continued, "the mutiny of the Congolese army; in 1961, the secession of Katanga; in 1964, the beginning of the rebellion in which the whole area was devastated. More than 30,000 small animals, sheep and goats were destroyed or killed by the rebels in the National Army, causing tremendous starvation."

But in that same year of 1964 and in 1965, Sam Vinton and Wayne Schoonover went back in with the reentry program and distributed food, clothing, blankets to overcome this problem.

Bunch added, "In 1967, there was the white mercenary mutiny in Bukavu and at that time Sam Vinton was at Kama. When everyone else was fleeing, he and the PAX men were building a 14-room elementary school at Kama. He was always active—a great overcomer."

Marie Vinton often employs a favorite method of informing her friends and supporters about their activities: "Notes from a Missionary's Diary." Some typical entries:

25

"Dec. 1—Two women and one man accepted the Lord in home prayer meetings.... Chief Peni Itula made his decision at the morning meeting.

"Len Andersons were at Lukula and reported seven who accepted the Lord and four returned to fellowship.

"Dec. 2—Mission village clean-up day. Everyone out working on yards, kitchens and houses.

"Dec. 5—A class of school boys had prepared some seed beds, so planted 25 packets of flower seeds.... Four women started making receiving blankets.... A mother brought her 18-month-old infant to see me.

"This is Baby Clinic Day, and there were 229 babies present. Flu is on the decrease here.

"Dec. 7—Left for weekend conference on the Shabunda road at Itangila. Girls sewing class between meetings.

"Dec. 8—Seven accepted the Lord this weekend.

"Dec. 9—Mission village looks grand—clean yards, trimmed hedges, freshly whitewashed houses.

"Dec. 15—Heard Billy Graham preach on radio—excellent reception.

"Dec. 17—Six Bible school students began working at our house, scraping oiled woodwork in living and dining rooms.

"Dec. 21—Group of 136 school boys with Yoana Wintita worked hard on new school building—four rooms—during our absence. When walls are dry, they will be plastered and whitewashed. School desks yet to be made."

Marie added, "Betty and I went to dispensary to help. Opened boxes of medicine.... Over 100 consultations each day; 80 leper patients receive their weekly treatments; more than 200 babies given antimalarial treatment each week.... Learned that 111 Kakumbu students are Christians.

"Dec. 25—Three nearby villages came to church here.... The workmen, masons, carpenters, mechanics, medical all took part and we had such a good service. Nine accepted the Lord Jesus."

Sam Vinton never hesitates to give credit to his "better half" for her part in the work. Sometimes in his reports to others he calls her Mama Vi, other times Marie.

"Rush call to the maternity," Sam once wrote for the mission magazine. "Got there too late. Baby born last night suddenly died. Called Marie to comfort the heartbroken mother. Had carpenter make little coffin. Our missionary life has its sorrows, too. How thankful we are that we can lead the sorrowful to Him who can comfort."

Lora Lee Spurlock, the pilot's wife, saw the Vinton motivation as "love for the Lord, passion for souls and very definite love for the

Africans. I've never known them during our 10-year acquaintance to act in a harsh, critical way.

"They always exemplify a sweet spirit of love and understanding, and they certainly have been a help to us in the trials and hard things that have come our way. They were always No. 1 on our list when we looked for advice.

"Their greatest accomplishment has been that they have grown more like Christ," she added. "They are beautiful people."

Typical of the heartfelt thanks that scores of nationals find ways to express was NyaKitingi, mother of Kitingi, 20-year-old son who was in a truck accident and had his foot amputated. Mama Vi helped the handicapped young man by giving him a sewing machine and teaching him to patch and help make clothes for invalids and others.

Though crippled herself, NyaKitingi knew she must find some way to thank Marie Vinton for her priceless help to her son. One day she arrived at the Vintons' door from several miles away, barely able to navigate. Mama Vi shook her head in disbelief as her visitor explained the purpose of her appearance.

"Mama Vi," NyaKitingi responded, "would it be right for me to *send* my thank offering to you? I just *had* to bring it myself, in person." And she handed Marie a large chicken.

Sometimes the appellation "wife of a missionary" has the meaning of simply a sympathetic helpmeet who keeps house and raises the children. Not so in the case of Marie Vinton—affectionately known to thousands of grateful Africans as Mama Vi. Hers indeed has been a ministry involving spirit, soul and body.

And because of her ministry—and that of her pioneer husband—there is hope for the future of Zaire.

CHAPTER 5

Zaire's One Great Hope

Tall, ebony black Andre Asumani, pastor of the church in Kama, smiled broadly as he welcomed his Sunday morning guests. One of the prize products of Sam and Marie Vinton's half-century of mission activity, the slightly stoop-shouldered African—now president of Grace Churches in Zaire—began at the bottom and climbed to the top.

From primary school, Asumani went on to the secondary school in Kama, then to Bible school two years, winding up as a graduate of the pastors' school after three more years. Then he became pastor of the large church in the village, eventually assuming leadership of all the Grace churches.

Now he talked quietly, yet forcefully, and the ears of 600 nationals who were crowded into the church building on this Sunday morning seemed strangely attuned to every word he uttered. Sam and Marie listened with special interest. With open windows, galvanized roof, concrete and brick walls, the church building boasts only long wooden benches—except for a half dozen chairs on the platform. The people seem happy to meet for upwards of two hours every week, and for special occasions as well.

"We're pleased to announce," Asumani says in his fluent Swahili, "that Sam Vinton Jr. and his wife Becky will be coming out in June (1980) with a team of young people under Grace Youth Ministries to help with our work in this area."

A murmur of excitement ripples through the audience as he continues.

"Becky will have classes to teach, and Sam Jr. will conduct a seminar for pastors and other church leaders. We are building a new girls' school, dividing up the work like Nehemiah did. We want that to be a good testimony of how to build."

Less than 100 yards away as the pastor speaks is the 2500-foot gravel airstrip that provides an invaluable lifeline for the station. Pastor Asumani recognizes a practical concern about the landing area.

28

"Pilot Jack Spurlock* has asked me to explain something to you," he begins with obvious earnestness. "Children, you must stay off the airstrip at all times, or someone might be killed. If you are on the strip when the plane comes in, it is impossible for the pilot to stop.

"From now on, this man here (pointing to one of the nationals) is in charge of the airstrip. When Mama Vi tells him the plane is coming in, he will be here to let us know. You must obey him and stay away from the strip. Any who disobey will be fined. From behind the ropes, you can watch the plane arrive and leave. Remember, this is our lifeline. Even your paper and pencils come that way."

Then the lanky, respected pastor points to another national. "This man is in charge of mail for the plane," he says. "You must get your letters to him on time for the return flight."

With the items of business out of the way, the service reverts to the performances of singing groups—of all sizes and varieties. With magnificent, untrained harmony, African voices burst into song. Samarie obviously relish the sterling performance. The nationals not only sing praises to God, but they also vocalize greetings to their American guests.

Zairian singers love to tell Bible stories vocally. Now a group sings about "The Story of Jonah." As they sing, their bodies sway sideways in unison. When the end of the story approaches, they begin to sing more quietly until only a whisper can be heard—all the while descending slowly to their seats during the final chords. Their loud volume and beautiful harmony, complete with excitement and enthusiasm, can hardly be surpassed in any American congregation—rarely equalled.

Half a dozen ensembles, following in rapid succession, add their beautiful melodies to the stirring service. Then comes the time most have been waiting for. Tall, suntanned Sam Vinton Sr., resplendent in a bright-colored, flowered sport shirt and plain slacks, stands behind the pulpit. Instant attention ensues as every ear strains to hear what Baba Vi has to say on this occasion.

After reading II Corinthians 5:17 from his Swahili Bible, the dramatic missionary-preacher calls on his audience to open their own Bibles and read the passage with him: "Therefore, if any man be in Christ, he is a new creation; old things are passed away; behold, all

---

*In 1980, Pilot Jack Spurlock was killed when the plane he was flying "threw a rod" and lost all power. He sighted a place where he thought he might land safely. But then, he saw the area was full of Africans. Not wanting to risk killing them, he headed for another, rougher area. Upon landing, the plane bounced into the air and came down nose first, burying the engine in the ground and killing "Jack" instantly. He was alone at the time.

29

things are become new."

Then follows a 25-minute sermon, punctuated often with apt gesticulations and hearty amens from his listeners. With great respect, they hang on every word and respond with amazing attentiveness.

Perhaps the most telling fact about the effectiveness of Sam and Marie Vinton's ministry is that the spoken word goes out from more than 200 pulpits in the Kama area every day of the week except Saturday, thanks to their many years of organizational ability. And the African people learn much about the Gospel from their songs, beautifully composed to tell a story easily understood by the people in their own culture and language.

"Indigenous methods work and are far superior in every way to present-day paternalistic methods," Sam Vinton declares. "The Kama group of churches is the only one in Eastern Zaire which does not have a church building constructed with outside funds. Local church groups of nationals have built all our church buildings with no outside financing."

Since 1958, Baba Vi continued, nationals have been members of the Field Council, with equal voting rights on matters of church policy, budget, projects and related items. Too, the missionaries believe the mission policy of not paying nationals to do the work of the church is 100 percent correct—and Pauline.

Vinton adds, "To support Christian school teachers in non-subsidized schools, while awaiting government takeover, has nothing to do with the mission policy of not paying church workers. We can certainly do that.

"Church-paid teachers must be Christian teachers who can and will be active in living a Christian testimony. They must actively participate in church services. They must see that the students attend at least the Sunday morning services. They must use the planned religion course—Bible stories, Scripture memory—in the schools' 'Religion Hours.' "

Vinton concludes: "Without such teachers we are doing 100 percent social-educational activity. We should establish a workable policy to provide equipment, but not on a non-participation basis. Kama church leaders should be asked to present their participation policy."

To help with the Bible school and pastors' school programs, the churches have built 17 duplexes to help house the students. Also, the Kama church provides food from their gardens.

"In everything we do," Vinton emphasizes, "let's insist on participation. Let's prove to the Africans that our main purpose in being here is the church. Together, we should get busy and prepare a church manual, then set up a committee to print it. We've had a ten-year setback because of uprisings and rebellion, but now it's time to move ahead."

On the subject of the Bible correspondence courses, which have been widely used in the area, Vinton asks, "What better method of reaching the whole church with the wonderful message of the grace of God?"

To cover each village church in the region requires about three years, but Sam Vinton goes about his rigorous work of planning the weekend safaris with the same zeal and determination with which he began them several years earlier.

Indicative of the type of church leaders the nationals have is Albert Mukula, first vice-president of the Grace Churches in Zaire, who walked 26 miles from his home village of Pene-Magu over rough terrain to attend a specially called meeting of the church board. He had given up his place on the safari truck for a sick person who needed to receive treatment at the Kama dispensary.

That spirit seems to typify the leadership of the national churches, learned no doubt from the sterling example set by Sam and Marie Vinton, who have a deep desire to grow in grace and to serve as salt and light in a needy land.

When Henry Sonneveldt, president emeritus of Grace Mission, Inc., shared his testimony as a layman at the Kama church on Sunday morning during our visit, he emphasized the need of lay participation in every aspect of church life. Then he challenged the national businessmen to become known for their honesty and integrity in business.

Concerned about the implementation of what they had heard, one of the lay leaders asked for an audience with Sonneveldt to discuss the matter. With missionary colleague Rich Nymeyer as interpreter, the 70-year-old mission leader met with four of the laymen at the church on a Saturday afternoon to answer their questions.

"What is the real work and responsibility of Christian laymen?" one of the Africans asked.

"Be an example to the people in the church and others in the community," Sonneveldt suggested, echoing the views of missionary pioneer Sam Vinton. "Be faithful in church attendance. Not only those in the church, but also those on the outside community are watching to see how Christians live, and if they don't live properly it can destroy their Christian testimony.

"As leaders in the church, you have the responsibility of training young men to bring their families into relationship with the Lord and with His church. Teach them just what it means to be members of the church."

Another layman asked about lay preaching on the part of those who have never studied the Bible.

"Perhaps the pastor should give a seminar on how to preach,"

Sonneveldt said. "You could develop lessons from the Bible, and learn how to share your testimony. When we speak for the Lord, He promises to put the very words in our mouths."

What activities could the laymen engage in besides having Bible study together?

"Remember to be sensitive and alert to the needs of the people, especially in your church fellowship, so you can reflect Christ's love to them. In addition, you might have special businessmen's meetings to which unbelievers could be invited. And you can plan activities to help others."

How can we learn to witness?

"Take notes of your pastor's messages, so that you will have that material plus your own personal witness to share with others. The layman has an advantage over the pastor as a witness, because the pastor as a paid worker is expected to be a witness."

A visitor to the Kama church comes away with one outstanding impression of the national believers: they love to sing praises to God; they do it beautifully, harmoniously, enthusiastically.

"We have used 20,000 songbooks in Swahili in less than three years," Vinton explains. "The Lord gave us most of these songs and hymns.

"These people love to dramatize Scripture, too," Baba Vi says. "And they are fine actors. Once we adapted Oswald J. Smith's booklet, 'The Man and the Well.' Paul Mali Sr. played the part of the man in the well, and they actually dug a big hole in the dirt just in front of the platform and pulpit."

After attempting to get out of his predicament by means of rituals, incantations, cowrie shell gifts and the like, the man in the well feels his dilemma is hopeless. Then comes the Lord Jesus Christ on the scene, played by one of the nationals.

While the onlookers listen and watch with suppressed excitement, the Saviour climbs down into the well with the fallen man. Suddenly he emerges from the hole, the man (Mali) on his shoulders, having been rescued amidst great shouting and applauding from the crowd. Baba Vi's invitation after the dramatic presentation meets with good success and scores respond.

Again, drama played an important part in the 50th anniversary celebration of the Vintons' ministry in Zaire. One of the nationals, a school teacher, had heard and read about "This Is Your Life"—erstwhile Ralph Edwards' television dramatization of the lives of celebrities.

Using makeshift curtains to open and close between acts, some 35 nationals portrayed the entire Vinton family, many of their colleagues and friends, in a warmly received skit that held the undivided attention of the overflow throng. Then came the awards presentation.

32

The Belgian Government gave the Vintons a medallion to honor their 50 years of sacrificial service. On behalf of the Grace Mission board, Sonneveldt presented a gold medal on a chain and gold watches to Sam and Marie. Then from himself and his wife, he gave them a gold platter inscribed: "To Rev. and Mrs. Samuel R. Vinton Sr., to commemorate 50 years' service for Christ, Belgian Congo, Zaire, Africa."

Several times earlier in their missionary career, the Vintons had received high honor (Order of Leopard, by Prince Charles of Belgium; knighted by King Leopold of Belgium, and knighted by President Mobutu of Zaire), and each time their response had been virtually the same:

"These are all wonderful things, but you people who have come out of darkness into the light of the Gospel mean more to us than all the decorations in the world. You are the lasting fruit of the gospel."

And Sam Vinton has another very meaningful way of expressing his feelings about the body of believers in Zaire. "The church is the mortar holding the villages together," he says.

The first church in Kama was built in 1928 with mud and sticks; its seating capacity, a mere 120. Eight years later, the first brick church was built and the capacity was 300. The men made the bricks while the women cut the wood needed in the structure, and together they supplied a serviceable leaf roof.

In 1946, the second brick church was built to seat 500, and the present structure built in 1960 holds 1200—"when they're solidly packed in," Vinton adds.

Proof of the pudding about the effectiveness of the Kama Bible Institute is the fact that close to 200 of its graduates now preach the gospel from the pulpits of Grace churches in Zaire.

Far from being a standstill operation, the Kama church is a thriving organism—with 111 new members having been welcomed into its fellowship on Easter Sunday of 1979 for example. And church membership is not as easy to attain as it is in most American churches. Six months of weekly membership classes are required, conducted by pastors and other church leaders. Some nationals are refused membership, if thorough evidence of regeneration is not apparent.

Not only the members but also the pastors face rigid requirements regarding their particular responsibilities. Called *wahubiri wa neno* (preachers of the Word) these men are held in high esteem by members of their flocks and by missionaries as well.

"No group of our people is so important as these *wahubiri*," Sam Vinton declares. "In the eyes of the world, they may not be worth much. Many of them have only a very meager education, as the world counts education, yet the future of this 'heart of Africa' depends on how faithful they are to their calling.

"These *wahubiri* are the great connecting link between peoples lost for generations in dense darkness and the true light, our Lord Jesus Christ."

Vinton then points out the chief tools employed by these national pastors. "They possess a copy of the New Testament in Swahili, a collection of stories from the Life of Christ, and a selection of Gospel songs.

"A few have copies of *Pilgrim's Progress,* and some have the whole Bible. Though simple and few, these tools in the hands of the *wahubiri* have proved to be dynamite—blasting a way into the very stronghold of Satan.

"The salvation of these Africans depends on these pastors. They, not the white missionaries, can and must reach the masses scattered in small villages over this vast land. They are God's shock troops, breaking through the enemy lines."

Vinton adds: "The life of these *wahubiri* is far from easy. They face opposition from many quarters, especially from the powerful secret sects such as the Bwami among the Warega. Witch doctors, idol worshippers and antagonistic village head-men withstand and plot against them.

"Some of these *wahubiri,* like the Apostle Paul, know the burning sting of a whiplash. Others have been cast into prison on flimsy pretexts. Some, secretly poisoned, have lost their lives. Yet these national pastors push forward unflinchingly, proclaiming the Gospel of the grace of God.

"Tito Molisho*, who holds the fort in P-Kusu, has faithfully served these people for many years, God has given him much fruit. Paulo Kia, his assistant and school teacher, has a fine enrollment of 29 in kindergarten, 70 in primary school and 59 in classes for adults. Church attendance is close to 300."

Baba Vi then tells you about other villages in his area. "Matayo, a big, husky, strong fellow physically, and a giant for God, preaches in Ngoma. He is an old soldier of the cross and has pioneered many outposts. Many trophies of grace have resulted from his faithfulness.

"Then Nedelema at Kiabene—our newest outpost. And what a record: 77 souls have come out of great darkness into the marvelous light of Christ . . . . Nedelema ate a 'taboo animal' and his life was

---

*Tito Molisho drowned in a plane accident in 1980. The plane he was riding in, with five others, lost power and the pilot had to land it in a river. One of the others, who just barely escaped the plane himself, tried to help Tito out but Tito, who couldn't swim anyway, just seemed to give up. He was heard praying, "Lord, I am coming! Receive me unto Yourself."

threatened, but even so he pushes on—preaching the Gospel in all boldness.

"At Katamba, the people once refused to even listen to the Gospel. But Asani persisted, and only a month ago eight received Christ in our special weekend meetings."

Albert Mukula, presently director of the branch Bible Institute at Pene Magu and vice-president of the executive committee, shared his testimony with the readers of *Outreach*. It sheds new light on the gospel ministry and its effectiveness in the area:

"I praise God for the way he saved me and called me to the ministry when I was a young man in the home of my mother and father. I was leading an ungodly life . . . . I was born among idol worshippers.

"One day Sam Vinton Sr. sent a teacher to a village near ours and I went to hear him. I also wanted to learn to read and write at the school he started, but my mother took me out of class to help take care of the children."

Mukula continued, "After my mother died, another teacher came to that village and I began classes . . . . I came to love my teacher, and when he told us of the judgment of God I received Christ as my Lord. Afterwards I really understood that God loved me and showed me His power."

One day Albert went with his father to trap fish. The elder Mukula was one to worship idols, and he said if his son wanted to catch fish he would have to cut himself on the wrist. This was a difficult situation, because Albert had been taught that he should worship no other gods, but he knew that he should honor his father.

"The Lord gave me the right words," Albert continued, "and when I told my father that we had been taught not to worship any other gods, he just laughed and said I wouldn't catch any fish. We put our traps in the water and next morning there was nothing in my father's traps, but there were fish in mine. I rejoiced to see that the Lord helps His own more than any idol can."

After several years of backsliding, Mukula renewed his relationship with the Lord and returned to His service in 1940. Three years later he was married, and in 1945 he was sent to pastor a church in Lubongola.

"God truly led me," Mukula said. "In January of 1955 I returned to my family and to my first church at Kama. Sam Vinton said that I should stay and work with his son, who was coming to work in the Bible school. We did work there as co-laborers.

"At the same time, I was a student in the Bible school for three years and in the pastor's school for two years. When they saw that I was able to direct the Bible school, they left the ministry in my hands."

The church in Zaire has a rich history. Organization of the Congo Protestant Council took place in 1925, and in 1970 the name was changed to *Eglise du Christ au Zaire* (Churches of Christ in Zaire).

By late 1977, the Kama group alone had 11,206 Christians in her churches. Some 306 villages in the area remain without a local church, so the great work of Sam and Marie Vinton and other missionaries in Eastern Zaire, while effective and fruitful, remains uncompleted.

CHAPTER 6

Safari, So Good

Heavy rains the night before, always devastating to the terrible roads in this area of Zaire, had delayed our departure from Kama for an hour. Now, at about 8:30 a.m., we prepared to begin our eventful journey, though this dubious writer lacked enthusiasm at the prospect.

Gala festivities in the village of Luyamba, 26 miles away, in celebration of the church's 45th anniversary there, would not begin until our arrival—probably around noon (averaging around eight miles per hour on the treacherous mudpaths sometimes called roads).

They would continue through the day and overnight, concluding early that second day (Thursday). Meanwhile, members of the safari—working together like clockwork after many years of team performance—began to take their places in the back of the truck.

Up front in the big Ford F600, six-wheel (dual tires on back) vehicle, Sam Vinton sits behind the wheel in his stocking feet—the better to "feel" his way into the various gears required for the back-breaking drive. Beside him is the safari superintendent, Madou, 35, mother of three children, who knows every hole in the road and actually does all the gear shifting while Baba Vi tenaciously grips the wheels and holds the truck to the road, such as it is.

Also in the front seat is Henry Sonneveldt, now on his twelfth trip to the Zaire field in behalf of Grace Mission—his major purpose this time as guide and companion for the writer.

Seated on wooden benches around the huge pile of equipment roped into the center of the truck loading space are the other members of the well-organized team, each with specific responsibilities that are taken care of efficiently all along the way.

Bitingo Yakobo serves as evangelist for the team. Most of the members act in multiple roles, practically all of them doubling as medical assistants on such safaris. Samweli Rafayele handles the keeping of records; Kyanga Louis and Malauza Yakobo major in medical roles. Mukuku Stefano's responsibilities are transport and water project.

37

Cinema, light plant and transportation duties fall to Fundisali Felix, who helps guide the truck across dangerous bridges by running ahead and motioning to Vinton so that he follows the safest path across the dubious supports. Fundisali's careful direction helps prevent the vehicle from plunging off the flimsy wooden structure into the waters below.

Maelena Maleuza handles cook and household duties; Rebeka Mbanki, medical and table; Maria, medical and preparation. Joining the special team members on this occasion were Rich Nymeyer and the writer, on hand to film and to report the trip. After a fluent prayer in Swahili by Pastor Bitingo, the entourage began with waving farewells to Mama Vi, Jane Nymeyer and other mission station personnel on hand for the occasion. The truck's loudspeaker then began to blare out Gospel songs as recorded by various church singing groups, thus alerting villagers and passersby that the Kama safari was approaching.

As we near the first of some seven or eight villages encountered along the way, excited children wave and shout as they run alongside the slow-moving vehicle. "Baba Vi! Baba Vi!" they yell, and Sam Vinton returns their greeting with a warm smile, a wave and a hearty "Yambo (hello)!"

On the relatively "safe" bridges, Fundisali hops off the back of the truck and positions himself on the other side to guide the driver across—somewhat like the signalling airport personnel does to steer an arriving plane into its proper spot at the terminal.

Culverts, huge round logs filling in as makeshift bridges in lesser ravines, are maneuvered without a guide. An occasional dangerous bridge, however, requires complete evacuation of the truck except for the driver and his assistant, who slowly, cautiously, prayerfully follow their guide's signalling across the treacherous structure. Other team members, meanwhile, walk cautiously across the bridge to await the safe crossing of the truck.

About an hour out of Kama, only one-third of the way to our destination, Baba Vi is flagged down by a villager waving frantically. A man inside the nearby mud hut has fainted. No one has any idea what his problem might be, so they call on Vinton for help. Responding immediately to the emergency, medical team members join the veteran missionary in the hut and administer reviving shots to the patient.

"If he is not completely well by the time we return this way tomorrow," Vinton explains, "we will take him with us back to Kama for treatment." Apparently a minor heart problem had temporarily laid him low.

Resuming the journey, cramped passengers hold firmly to stable parts of the truck in order to minimize the frequent jolts caused by the road. Soon the truck comes to a halt again, this time to drop off salt and soap which had been ordered by officials of the particular village on a recent trip to the Kama station.

After one additional village stop, to pull an abscessed tooth, the missionary motorists arrived at Luyamba, where a throng of several hundred villagers had gathered as a welcoming committee. Hoisting their special guests atop their shoulders, the shouting, singing, exuberant nationals walked triumphantly through the length of the village—joined along the way by enthusiastic crowds.

Signs of welcome also called attention to the historic occasion: the 45th anniversary of the Luyamba church, now a thriving entity of its own, thanks to the much earlier efforts of Sam and Marie Vinton.

Arriving at the pastor's residence, by comparison a palace of its own—though extremely modest by American standards—the excited villagers deposited their charges at the door. While team members prepared a quick lunch for the weary travelers, Baba Vi wasted no time in proceeding to the village dispensary just across the way, where some 200 patients had waited eagerly—some for many hours.

Assistants carried cots from atop the truck, placing them in otherwise bare rooms, where the visiting guests would spend the night. Bedding and mosquito netting soon were in place. Meanwhile, outside, the incessant bleating of goats punctuated the silence. An occasional blasting of a gun gave further evidence that the big celebration had begun.

Shortly, the loud cheers of villagers just outside our modest "dining room" announced the arrival of the big man himself, Chief Funga Funga, head over 41 villages, who had walked 15 miles to be a part of the festivities. Seven subchiefs from surrounding villages joined him for the occasion.

Learning that the travelers had brought 20 Swahili Bibles with them, some 50 or more nationals began to beg Sam Vinton for copies, offering up to several weeks' wages for a copy of the prized book. Many wanted to leave their money with Baba Vi in exchange for a Bible to be delivered at some future date. Uncertain as to the arrival of additional copies, Vinton had to turn the whole problem over to Andre Asumani, whose broad, lanky shoulders could help him decide the most equitable distribution of available copies.

On typical safaris, especially the weekend type, the host churches are responsible to provide food and lodging for up to 2,000 guests, meaning simply that their already crowded mud huts become more cramped for space than ever. Local church members prepare the program, learn new songs and Scripture verses, and work for days to prepare food, make oil and cut firewood.

For a special occasion such as this, however, more elaborate preparations had been made for weeks in advance by a committee

39

appointed for the purpose. Now the fruit of their combined labors began to be realized.

Opening ceremonies commenced out in the open, in the center of the village, where thousands of onlookers had gathered around a roped-off area. A crude but effective loudspeaker gave sufficient amplification for the tremendous throng.

Scores of VIP's—village leaders, pastors, church officials and visiting guests—occupied a makeshift reviewing stand, with six long rows of chairs situated under a temporary leaf shelter that kept the hot African sun from broiling their bodies.

Colorful dancers in tribal dress performed at great length, their graceful gyrations followed by gymnastic feats and interspersed with appropriate comments by church and village leaders. All the while, talking drums announced to nearby villagers that the big ceremony had begun. At the very outset, appropriate reverence and respect accompanied the singing of "We Are Zairois" (the national anthem which speaks of peace, justice, work).

After lengthy ceremonies, attendants removed the ropes and motioned the crowds further back so that everyone in the reviewing stand might watch the next big feature. Then two barefooted soccer teams, one local and the other from a neighboring village, ran single file in front of the stand enroute to the adjacent playing field. Two or three sizeable trees, a goat or two, and several chickens—decorating the terrain—hardly bothered the agile athletes at all. A scoreless tie seemed a fitting conclusion to a hardfought contest.

All the while, an excited, would-be Jim McKay, Olympic announcer—using a make-believe mike formed out of an ancient phonograph—described the play-by-play action with all the fervor of the most rabid American sportscaster. Apparently conditioned to such extemporaneous performances, the nationals paid little or no attention to the budding announcer.

A tour of the village revealed a primary school with 379 students; a secondary school with 179 students; a brick kiln in which 3,600 bricks were being made at the time; windowless classrooms with crude wooden benches and desks, plus a masonite blackboard in fair condition; an outdoor forge to make spears and other sharp instruments.

On that Wednesday evening, the church building itself—founded and built some 45 years earlier under Sam Vinton's super-vision—looked as if it would burst at the seams as hundreds of villagers and nearby guests jammed every corner of the well-constructed building. Scores of others peered through bamboo-slit windows. Team members already had strung light bulbs from front to back in the primitive sanctuary to provide the only lighting the nationals had seen for some time.

Although the total village population numbered only 497, several thousand people came for the two-day celebration, and the extended-family concept would be severely put to the test. Cramped huts could be seen everywhere.

Though the church building barely holds its 247 members, more than 400 have crowded into and around the structure within a short time after the service begins. Obviously well-planned and thoroughly rehearsed for the occasion, the program moved smoothly without introduction of the various components. Sam Vinton's warm smile reflected his joy at the progress of the Luyamba believers.

A group of 25 or 30 men and women recited Scripture in unison. Several musical ensembles stood in their places, one after another, and presented their Gospel songs in Swahili—again swinging and swaying gracefully as they sang—then gradually lessening their volume as they slowly descended to their seats.

Strong, articulate, respected Pastor Andre Asumani then began to speak. "Praise God for His help in carrying out our program," he began. "This is evidence of God's blessing on the work. If we get in God's order, things will go right. We must build on the Bible.

"What's in this Bible—the living Word—is Christ. Christ said, 'When I go I will come again.' He is everywhere. The same God who gave His people their faith is our God."

Asumani's grateful mentor, Sam Vinton, listened attentively from his wooden chair behind the makeshift pulpit, punctuating the speaker's remarks with hearty amens. His prized pupil had learned his lessons well.

"Without Christ," Pastor Andre continued, "your wealth, your wisdom don't mean anything. Wealth and wisdom without Christ bring war and greed. You Christians, when the Bible says don't do this or that—and you do it—you become an enemy of God and the church.

"Christ said, 'If you take My Word, you will love it—you will do it.' If you refuse to obey God's Word, you are a rebel—an enemy. We are to be His ambassadors. Let's stand on the Word!"

After the formal service, truly a spiritual blessing to many, a murmur of expectancy gripped the overflow throng. A movie screen was put in place, and lights extinguished as the projector began to show the first of three films brought along especially for the occasion.

Incongruously, an Abbott and Costello comedy flashed on the screen, minus the American soundtrack, but augmented by an African announcer present in person to describe as best he could just what was taking place. Loud laughter sounded like sweet music to the ears in a remote jungle village where laughter was a rare

41

commodity.

As the first film concluded to loud applause, the second began—a depiction of the famed basketball team, the Harlem Globetrotters. And again the self-appointed announcer sought to describe the action. Gales of laughter swept through the audience as the strange antics continued.

Quiet reigned as the third and final film flashed on the screen: "The Healing of the Nobleman's Son." Based on John 4 and its familiar story, the movie captured the serious attention of the nationals. By this time, close to 600 people had come within earshot if not eyeview of the proceedings. Amusingly, two sturdily built men could be seen sharing one ordinary folding chair, each clinging to a small corner of the seat, hands on knees for the purpose of steadying.

An exciting evening concluded, the jubilant villagers began to wend their ways to totally dark mud huts. For a few unforgettable minutes, they had left their meager surroundings and enjoyed a taste of "civilization."

Thursday morning, at the crack of dawn, Baba Vi had already made a fire just outside our overnight residence— "the best way to have a one-to-one witness with the people," he explained. Sure enough, an elderly African man—once a traveling companion of the chief national evangelist in the area and also head of the building committee—quickly joined Vinton and several others around the fire.

"Please," the old man began, pointing his remarks to Baba Vi, "don't take a short-cut to heaven and lead us in a roundabout way."

Baba Vi laughed aloud at the quaint suggestion. "No," he promised. "We'll all get there the same way, by faith in Jesus Christ."

Both Vinton and his attentive listener spoke in fluent Swahili, while an increasing crowd of nationals—both young and old—began to gather around the fire.

"Many Christians fail to witness," the old man observed perceptively, his wizened features barely distinguishable in the faint light of the fire.

"Yes," Baba Vi countered, "lots of people *see* your life much clearer than they *hear* those who preach a sermon."

Noting Vinton's use of a battery-operated electric shaver, in the semi-darkness around the fire, the old man pointed to the modern convenience.

"Men who make that kind of luxury help take people's thoughts from God," he said.

Again, Vinton smiled broadly as he replied. "A good person with a good heart learns to appreciate God more than ever, even with the luxuries. The same thing can be good for one person, bad for another—if he covets."

Moving rapidly from one subject to another, the elderly African continued his conversation.

"You taught me not to love money," he said. "Now I let my wife handle it, so I won't get to love it."

Baba Vi chuckled. "It's hard to use money and not love it," he said. "Sometimes people love their own money and other people's money, too. People who are hoarding money don't help others, but there are many people who help others with their money."

While Vinton stoked more wood on the fire, his listener made an observation. "There are three blind men in this village," he said, "but nobody brings any food to them. Three goats are killed during the celebration, but nothing is given to them." Then, changing the subject abruptly, "We want lights around here."

Baba Vi nodded. "And you can have them. Get your committee together; it's not too far to a mining town where you can get the necessary supplies."

Observing one of the national pastors standing by, the old man turned aside for a moment and directed a comment to him. "If you walk back to your village instead of riding," he said, "you will have an opportunity to witness and shake hands with many people along the way."

During the momentary diversion, Vinton turned to his two-way shortwave radio for the usual morning communication with the Kama base. Soon Mama Vi and Jane Nymeyer were on the line.

The old African beamed broadly as he heard the voice of Marie Vinton greeting him warmly via radio. Jane delivered a message to Pastor Asumani. Then an exchange of weather reports revealed that Kama, only 26 miles away, had experienced a heavy rainstorm after the team's departure, continuing on into Thursday. Meanwhile, Luyamba had been favored with fine weather for the big celebration.

"No rain?" Jane said quizzically. "You must have a special umbrella from God!" And indeed the dry weather had made possible the successful outdoor ceremonies that had attracted thousands of villagers.

Their radio conversation ended, the old man resumed his observations and questions. "Pastor Asumani should have one of these two-way radios," he said. Baba Vi laughed in assent.

When the elderly African asked about the dilemma of unanswered prayer, Vinton reminded him about Paul and his thorn in the flesh. God had told the apostle, "My grace is sufficient for thee."

Turning to the several national pastors who by now had joined the group around the fire, the old man commented: "You preachers be sure to get all this good teaching from Baba Vi, so you can teach it to us after he goes."

Excusing himself for a moment, Baba Vi turned his attention to a young man about 15 obviously in pain with an abscessed tooth. With

43

the whole outdoors as his dental office, Vinton used his forceps and pulled the tooth. Greatly relieved, the boy walked away. Then an elderly woman with a similar problem needed his attention. She too felt relief after the offending tooth had been pulled.

"That's why I love this life," Baba Vi observed to the writer as he returned to his chair beside the fire. "You can help people." And that indeed seems to summarize the life and ministry of Samarie.

Meanwhile, the old man wanted to make one final point before the crowd left the flickering fire and dispersed. "We worshipped god in the dark before (worshipping idols at the shrine)," he said. "Since Baba Vi came, we worship God in the light."

As a small crowd of about 100 Africans, mostly women—some with their pre-school children, gathered in the church for a Thursday morning service, Vinton observed to the writer: "I try to take Pastor Asumani with me on our safaris at least once every three months."

Suddenly a recognizable tune, "Down at the Cross"—though in offbeat Swahili rhythm—rumbles through the audience, picking up volume as the singing progresses. Soon the singers change to the Kirega dialect. Within half an hour, the crowd has grown to around 400. Musical numbers comprise most of the opening portion of the service.

A closing challenge by Pastor Asumani reminds the people: "The white man had the light before we did, but now we should go on and serve Christ. Get awake! Don't sleep! You are a Christian now. Do something about it! We fail many times because we limit God.

"Your faith should be greater than Mary because you have the Scriptures. You have more knowledge than Peter. He didn't know what we have in this Word (holding up his Swahili Bible)."

A justifiably proud Baba Vi interprets Asumani's remarks for the writer, somewhat animatedly though quietly, with an occasional chuckle at the pastor's asides.

"Christ specifically says we are not to be sinners," Pastor Andre continues. "There is no real fellowship between Christians and unbelievers. You can't have fellowship with God if you are a drunkard or a thief."

After reading II Corinthians 6:14-17, he adds, "We have a foundation in this church. Baba Vi told us to build a strong foundation. We didn't really want to work, but he stood there and made us do it. Now we are glad he did.

"The work isn't finished yet. We still need window frames in our church building. Don't ever say our work is finished. What lies ahead is greater than what is behind. You Christians, you pastors, you elders, you men and women, don't think we have finished with our work.

"We are starting with a new vision. We want to finish the work.

Check your own lives. Forget drinking and stealing. Don't do things you shouldn't do. We are made in God's likeness. The Bible says the fear of the Lord is the beginning of wisdom."

What had been announced in advance as a half-hour service, in typical African fashion proved elastic in length—something over an hour—before the crowd moved out and over to the ceremonial field for the concluding activities.

Early in the public program, Sam Vinton was introduced to the great Thursday morning throng, again outside the roped-off area, and loud cheers greeted the missionary statesman as he approached the microphone.

One of missions' great communicators, the articulate Baba Vi wasted no time in getting to the heart of his message. He had something important he wanted to say, and he felt it could be said in a few minutes' time.

"Let's go forward," he began. "Stand strong in the faith. As Paul said in Philippians, we are to 'press toward the mark for the prize of the high calling of God in Christ Jesus.' God's message today is, 'Go forward!' " His ringing challenge evoked a hearty response.

As the ceremonies continued, one pastor came forward and read Psalm 146 in Swahili. Then another read Psalm 147. As if to emphasize that deeds must follow words, two nationals carried large (55-pound) bags of salt to a spot near the rostrum, ready for distribution to needy villagers. Then a third African pastor read Psalm 148.

Called on again because of his prominent place in the church of Zaire, Andre Asumani proved equal to the challenge.

"Our aim is to know God," he said, "to please Him. You can't develop a country by just waiting for the rains to come down. It is a sad thing to see a lot of young people who have no work.

"A village without a church turns bad. Baba Vi gave the pastors here teaching, schools and medical services. Now our medical work is lost. I am asking you chiefs, what plans do you have for developing your villages in 1980?" In typical African fashion, the dynamic speaker changed subjects often, as if eager to cover a wide range of subjects in a limited span of time.

Then, turning to the head man in the area, Pastor Asumani continued: "The big chief left his village in the rain and arrived here in the rain after walking 15 miles, because he wanted to be a part of this celebration.

"Baba Vi encouraged us and helped us and strengthened us, and that's why we have our big church there (pointing to the imposing structure less than 200 yards away)."

A lengthy roster of introductions then took place, including a former chief of the village; a number of old-timers who pioneered in

Luyamba, and other former villagers. A number of onetime residents who had moved away to succeed and earn good salaries in other parts of the country, unable to attend the ceremonies, had sent money to distribute to church leaders and village heads.

Then came the distribution of the prized 20 Swahili Bibles. Pastor Andre had decided they should be given to certain chiefs and church leaders. As each one received his coveted copy of the Word of God, several enthusiastic nationals hoisted the recipient atop their shoulders and carted him around the open area amidst much laughter and loud applause.

When the chief of Luyamba received his Bible, he held it aloft and shouted so all could hear: "I have something here better than all the money in the world," an obvious reference to the distribution of funds moments earlier.

In one item of business conducted by the chiefs and subchiefs during the two-day festivities, they voted unanimously to give to Sam Vinton and the Kama mission a fine building in Esagu, about 20 miles from Kama, that had formerly belonged to the government but now was empty. A health center would be located there.

A weary but rejoicing entourage, their mission completed, left Luvamba early Thursday afternoon and three hours later relaxed in the beauty and comfort of Kama mission station. In typical Mama Vi style, she was on hand at the dispensary as the truck pulled up, a cold pitcher of Kool-Aid on hand to greet the thirsty travelers.

Such safaris are a way of life for Sam and Marie Vinton, and one could hardly imagine a more effective way to reach the people of the villages—both physically and spiritually. For that very reason, Baba Vi overlooks age and weariness as he plans ahead for at least one safari a week far into the future. As long as the needs exist, and he knows about them, Sam Vinton will be there with his team.

Asked about such bad roads as had been seen and felt between Kama and Luyamba, Vinton laughed. "Those are the best roads in the whole area," he said.

In earlier years, a younger Vinton and his team would carry all the equipment and walk to their target villages. Now, with a suitable truck available and a wider field to cover, they make excellent use of the somewhat quicker method by truck.

Far from being hit-and-miss operations, the safaris feature a theme for each year, and local pastors and village leaders plan their weekend activities around that theme. For 1979, the theme was "Edification," and songs, memory verses and messages centered on that subject. "Work" was chosen as the 1980 topic.

Because of the gas shortage, which apparently has affected every part of the world—even the remote jungles of Africa—some of the safaris are being strung together in such a way that Vinton and his team may be gone for as long as 10 days to two weeks at a time. On their latest trip to Kindu, for example, the team held six safaris in 15 days.

"People are hungry," Baba Vi explains, "not only physically but spiritually. They want us; they need us. How can we turn them down?"

Sam Vinton's teams are so well trained that, in his absence—mostly when he can't be in but one place at a time—his national pastors take over the responsibility of leadership. He has great confidence in their ability, both as leaders and as preachers. Usually up to 15 pastors might be at a given safari conference; for a special occasion like the anniversary celebration of Luyamba, 25 ministers were on hand.

Baba Vi has not missed a safari appointment in ten years, but he has had some narrow escapes. On one of his weekend expeditions, as he crossed a narrow, wobbly bridge, Vinton heard a terrible crack beneath him. In a moment's time, the truck had plunged through the bridge and landed on the bank of a river. Nearby villagers pulled out all 27 passengers and righted the truck. Miraculously, not one suffered injury.

With true African hospitality, the people in nearby villages put them all up for the night, and early next morning the trip resumed.

At one period, the safaris began at 4 a.m. so that the team would arrive in the host village around 7 a.m. ready to work. Later experience proved that an evening departure time usually is best, so that not only the team but also visiting villagers might all be on hand by next morning ready for a full day of activity.

Martha, Vinton's safari cook, is a former TB patient whose case has since been arrested. She has earned her medicine in that way. Similarly, Madou, the capable safari superintendent, once had TB which has been arrested, thanks to the medical ministry of Samarie Vinton.

Always a vital part of the safari program is the film ministry. In addition to the three movies shown at Luyamba, another favorite is "The Life of Christ." "Many have broken down and wept at the reality of Christ on the cross," Vinton reports.

Such modern luxuries as baths and showers are not totally forgotten on the journeys to outlying villages. With a screen of leaves around them, out under the open sky, team members sometimes are able to enjoy a makeshift shower—employing a large basin of water to rinse off the foamy soap. A simple chair serves as repository for towel and soap.

Meals on safari are erratic, adaptable to conditions in the villages being visited. Sometimes they are served twice a day, at appropriate break times; on occasion, there is time for only one meal a day. But eating always is secondary to the primary purpose and activities of the kusanyikos.

In a 1975 report to the constituency through *Outreach* magazine, Vinton shared his evaluation of the safari ministry:

"The greatest missionary of all times, the Apostle Paul, is the outstanding example of the mobile missionary. He wrote: 'In journeyings often . . . '; 'I have traveled many weary miles.'

"An old Chinese proverb says, 'Go to the people, live among them, learn from them, love them.'

"It was not until after the rebellions here in Zaire that our eyes were really opened to the tremendous needs of the people living in the more than 100 villages of the Kama area. This became a call to us to go 'mobile'—to go to the people, to help them meet their needs, spiritual, physical and material, right in their own home village."

Vinton added, "To become mobile, we organized a team composed of evangelistic, medical, developmental—and in some cases educational—workers. Our plan of action: to *reach* the people:

"First, through our weekend evangelistic series of meetings in which eight to twelve churches participate, Gospel singers and church groups provide an hour or so of special singing each meeting; visiting pastors bring messages from the Word; films and slides follow each evening meeting."

Vinton then emphasized the medical ministry. "Secondly, by creating health centers with (1) pre-natal clinics for expectant mothers; (2) baby clinics for the 'under-fives'; (3) infertility clinics for the childless couples; (4) family planning clinics; (5) curative medicine—providing treatment and transportation to Kama; (6) preventive medicine—with war on malaria by prophylaxis, on intestinal parasites through hygiene, safe drinking water, etc.; immunization; natural vitamins.

"Thirdly, by providing a purchasing service through which orders can be placed and goods delivered on our regular safari. Kama is the only source of supply for most of the villages."

Describing prerequisites for area participation, Vinton said, "A village—to qualify for a Health Center—must have three to five villages nearby. The people must be willing to clear the site, gather the building materials from the forest, construct the five-room building and provide food and lodging for our team.

"Because of these safaris, the number of in-patients at Kama has dropped from 90 to 30—a tremendous savings in money, medicines and time.

"Nearly 200 leper patients have been released from the settlement and moved back to their homes, since they now receive treatment at our health centers."

Vinton then proceeded to describe a typical schedule for the weekend events, "After our safari prayer by Pastor Bitingo, we are off to the sound of good Gospel singing over the loudspeaker mounted on the cab.

"Ten kilometers (about seven miles) out, we stop at a dangerous bridge. Planks are all gone. Passengers cross on foot. We drive across on the timbers—dangerous when wet and slippery.

"Stops are made in villages along the way to let off passengers. A mother with a new baby from the maternity ward brings people running toward her with great rejoicing."

An earlier visit to the 45th anniversary site featured medical activities. "At Luyamba the patients are lined up waiting for us. Five tables, eight chairs and basins of water—all are ready. No cool waiting room, no comfortable chairs, but everyone is happy that we have arrived.

"After singing and prayer, we are ready for work. My table is set before the open window, our medical chests are opened and my assistants, Mandelena and Rebeka, have the pills and ampules ready."

Vinton added, "The patients come one by one and describe their symptoms. As they talk, I prescribe—or reach out my hand to one of the girls who drops the proper pills or ampules into it.

"It takes from two to four hours per clinic. When the patients have been taken care of, we move over to the examination room. The last lineup, from 3 to 15 patients, have abscessed teeth needing attention.

"Transport members, meanwhile, are loading the medical chests and other supplies, and we are off to our next village."

With little concern for rest and relaxation, Vinton and his entourage maintained their hectic pace. "Our next stop, an hour later, is at Mukulukusu. We follow the same routine as at Luyamba. We are going to be late because of hauling those timbers for the bridge. Fundisali checks the lines to see if he must set up the portable light plant. He decides we'll be through before dark.

"We drive for an hour to Lukuka. People welcome us but are disappointed we arrived too late to meet with them in the church. We sit and talk with the chief, the pastors and the school teachers.

"Our accommodations are on village level—stick and mud house with leaf roof and earth floors, but clean and furnished with table and chairs. We have our own camp cots."

Vinton added, "Tomorrow we'll have a clinic here at Lukuka, check on the work at the wells and at the brick press, where the village people are making bricks to build a new school building. Then we go to Kierlo for the weekend meetings.

"This gives you an idea of the work. We have anywhere from 200 to 600 patients per day, 500 to 1500 for the weekend meetings. Through the village church, the team is involved in the lives of individuals, of families and of communities."

When Pastor Yakobo Bitingo, chairman of the department of evangelization, took part in six successive safaris to outlying villages—totalling almost one thousand miles over the treacherous roads—he reported 235 adults and 394 children as having made decisions for Christ, and 13 believers restored to fellowship with the Lord.

In 1976, Sam Vinton appealed to his American supporters and friends to pray for a special safari effort:

"Pastor Asumani and a team of 18 church leaders have just come back from a 15-day trek through a new large area which our Grace churches of Kama have been invited to occupy.

"They made plans for our mobile team to spend a week in this new region—with 67 villages and three big centers along a 100-mile stretch of the Kama-Kindu road."

Vinton added, "We plan to leave Kama April 27, and this will be our first safari into that area. Already 21 pastors from Kama have moved into the area—'missionaries from the Kama church.'

"Our main objectives will include evangelistic meetings in five centers and three days of meetings at Lumuna—the first campaign of this type ever held in the area."

Detailing the actual schedule, Vinton continued: "Bill Bunch and Pastor Katamea will head up the child evangelism and Youth for Christ meetings.

"Secondly, we will help select sites on which churches and parsonages can be built.

"Thirdly, members of the medical team will hold clinics in each of the villages.

"Fourthly, we will have a tree-planting ceremony at each church plot, and set out oil palms, citrus trees and avocados, among others.

"Finally, we will repair some broken down pumps and replace others with new pumps."

Vinton concluded: "We are printing a special song sheet with ten songs to be used during the meetings. Sam Jr. will write, and have printed, a special tract for the safari.

"We are reminded," Sam Sr. wrote in his closing appeal for prayer support, "that 'we are not fighting against people made of flesh and blood, but against persons without bodies—the evil rulers of the unseen world, those mighty satanic beings and great evil princes of darkness who rule this world, and against huge number of wicked spirits in the spirit world,'" (Ephesians 6:12 LB).

One of the most significant ministries in all of Zaire is that of these safaris, for they accomplish both spiritual and physical good beyond measure. Unquestionably, these missionary journeys will continue as long as Sam and Marie Vinton have breath to insure their perpetuation.

And, missionary colleagues will not soon forget their stirring experiences with Samarie on the world's worst roads.

CHAPTER 7

Riots, Rebellions and Roads

During the Simba rebellion in 1964, Kama lay in the area taken captive by the rebels. The missionaries had long since fled to Bukavu. Word came one day that the government soldiers were recapturing the area, and travel to Shabunda—and even to Kama—might be possible. Sam Vinton, "chomping at the bit and rarin' to go," asked missionary colleague Ernie Green to accompany him.

"I couldn't say I was rarin' to go," Green said. "I did want to see all of the African pastors, evangelists, elders and people, but I was leery of the information which had come.

"Were the government soldiers *really* being successful? Was it actually *safe* to go to Shabunda? How much farther toward Kama could we *really* go before running into rebel soldiers? I was certain they would like nothing better than to kill Baba Vi, and since I would be along, that meant me, too."

Green remembered that "none of these things moved Baba Vi. Day after day, he worked at getting things ready, purchasing all sorts of things—soap, cloth, hoes, machetes—to take along to Kama, *if* we could get there.

"At 4:00 o'clock one afternoon, the two trucks (an International six-passenger pickup and a Bedford two-ton) roared into the yard. 'C'mon, Ernie, let's go!' Baba Vi shouted, as he hurried to tell Mama Vi goodbye."

What a horrible time to start out, Green thought to himself. "Knowing it would take the rest of the day, all night and most of the next day to get to Shabunda, it seemed ridiculous to leave at 4:00 in the afternoon," he said. "Yet, leave we did!

"The first two hours weren't bad as we traveled in daylight and along the fairly good road going out from Bukavu toward the great Kivu Forest. At dusk, our caravan pulled to a stop along the road to eat our rice and greens. Baba Vi drank one of the small cans of condensed milk he always carried along on such safaris. (It seemed to me he just about lived on condensed milk most of the trip!)

"Entering the forest and driving *that* road was something else. It always had been classed as the worst road in Africa, if not in the world. The holes, rocks and mud were indescribable. We had to creep along at 5-10 miles an hour."

Green recalled that he "gave up counting the number of times we got bogged down in seemingly bottomless seas of mud—at times, it seemed, a block long. The amazing thing was that the International four-wheel drive, six-passenger pickup would actually plow through it.

"The big truck, loaded to the gills, would invariably get stuck every time. The first time it happened, I could hardly believe my eyes when Baba Vi drove the pickup through the sea of mud and then, when the big truck got bogged down in it, he backed into the mud, hooked onto the truck sunk in mud up to its axles and *pulled it out!* One section of the road took us 12 hours to go 56 miles."

As Baba Vi drove on and on into the night, Green and the African in the cab with him tried desperately to get some sleep while the truck jostled, jerked and bounced.

"About noon the next day," Green said, "we pulled into Ikozi Mission Station—140 miles in 20 hours. The Africans were overjoyed to see some missionaries, but we had precious little time to spend with them. I knew them real well and hated to move on, but we had to head for Shabunda. Arriving there in the early evening, we finally had a chance to go to bed and get some sleep.

"Sam and I had not traveled like this before, so I didn't know what to expect. The next morning, I kept waiting for him to say we would go to early morning chapel with the African Christians. Finally, I went alone."

Green continued, "If we thought the Africans had been excited to see us when we pulled in the night before, now they could hardly contain themselves. A missionary was actually in their service with them again! Baba Vi joined us before it was over, and we gave Christian greetings and love to all. He gave them a 'pep talk,' too.

"On our way—in the direction of Kama! Baba Vi began stopping at each village to ask if it were safe to go on and if the rebels had been routed at Kama. Each time, they assured us it was safe to go on, so *on we went!"*

The further they went, the more they saw the havoc wrought by the rebels—53 villages completely burned out; in one village 163 homes burned to the ground, in another 200. The people had fled the year before at garden planting time. Their rice and peanuts, ready to plant, remained in the houses so had been burned up.

The villagers had been hiding in the forest six months, living on greens, roots and other things they saw the chimpanzees eat. Now they were returning to their burned-out villages to rebuild, but actually there was no food or medicine. As Sam Vinton reviewed the

53

carnage, the sick (especially the children whom he loved dearly), and the great needs all around him, the "hurt" on his face showed how much he cared for these people—*his* people.

A short way from Kama, the road was blocked—not by rebels, but by mobs of Christians from Kama and nearby villages. For the last mile, the trucks inched along as swarms of people walked in the road and surrounded the vehicles. They were shouting, yelling, weeping for joy, singing hymns—demonstrating their warm welcome to the missionaries. Finally, they insisted that Baba Vi get out of the truck, and they carried him on their shoulders the rest of the way to Kama.

Once there, bedlam broke loose. *Baba Vi had returned!* The people went wild with joy and excitement.

Government soldiers had, indeed, taken charge at Kama. In fact, they had a rebel prison there, with 60 people apprehended. It had not been the policy of the Congolese Army nor the rebels to take any prisoners, but rather to shoot them all. But the Army was now urging the rebels to come out of hiding, promising that later there would be trials. Some of the rebel prisoners were cutting the grass around the Vinton home. The forest around Kama was full of rebels.

"We won't stay long, Ernie," said Baba Vi. "It's pretty dangerous here. We'll just get the truck unloaded, stay a couple of hours and head out."

Green was relieved, but about an hour later Vinton came to him saying, "Ernie, what do you think? Should we stay all night and leave in the morning?"

"Baba Vi," Green responded, "I don't think we should stay all night. It is just too dangerous with the forest full of rebels and others in prison. I think we ought to start back."

"You're probably right," called Vinton, as he took off for another duty. Just before dark, he approached Green again. "Ernie, we're going to stay. The soldiers assure me it will be safe."

The African truck driver slept on the front porch, with a huge monkey wrench by his head, presumably to protect himself and the missionaries if any rebels approached.

Early the next morning, an African pastor (Albert Mukula) came to Green. "SaKatumbi (Ernie's African name), I asked for, and received, permission from the Adjutant for us to have a meeting with the rebels in prison. Will you go with me and preach to them?"

Baba Vi and Green rejoiced at the opportunity, and Mukula and Ernie went to the old print shop which was doubling as a prison. Knowing that some of them might be shot as rebels, Green pointed out to them that *no one*—rebel, soldier, missionary—can come unto God the Father except through Jesus Christ the Son.

Sam Vinton, meanwhile, scurried around giving last-minute instructions, helping Africans in need and preparing the trucks for

54

leaving. A huge crowd of Africans, weeping and wailing, came to say farewell to the missionaries.

When they reached Shabunda, Baba Vi allowed Green and the African truck driver to take the truck and go to Katanti, the mission station where Ernie's family had worked for nearly ten years before joining Grace Mission. Sam knew how his colleague longed to see old friends there.

As the Kama folks had gone wild at seeing Baba Vi, so the Katanti folks went wild at seeing SaKatumbi. The shouting, weeping, laughing and hugging went on way into the night.

Baba Vi had agreed that if the Green piano was still intact and usable, it could be loaded onto the truck and taken to Bukavu. He really loved the Green's daughter, Pat, and wanted her to have the piano.

An African family with ten children had lived in the dorm with it. The rebels and the Congolese had "camped" in the house, so the piano was filthy with scummy, greasy dirt. Deep burns appeared at one end where someone had set a cigarette. Amazingly, a fairly good tone still could be heard.

Placing the piano in the truck with its back up against the cab, workmen nailed 2x4's around it on the floor of the truck so the instrument couldn't shift, then covered it with blankets and nailed another 2x4 from one side of the truck to the other in front of the keyboard. Forest vines helped to tie the piano securely to the cab. Whenever the truck fell into a hole, the piano of course plunged with it, though the instrument did not budge.

When Green met Baba Vi at the crossroads the next morning, to complete the return trip to Bukavu, he found the veteran missionary delighted to see the piano. He knew what a blessing it would be to his young friend, Pat.

Except for that same horrible road of holes, rocks and mud, the trip back was uneventful. Eight days after starting out, the missionaries pulled into the driveway of the Bukavu guest-house—their home. Their grateful wives joyfully hugged and kissed them—dirt, grime, whiskers and all!

Though Ernie Green was worn to a frazzle and bone-weary, Sam Vinton seemed to be his old "peppy" self, despite the dangerous, grueling, eight-day ordeal. "Even considering the grace of God on his behalf, one wonders *how he does it,*" Green said.

Another time, Sam and Marie Vinton, their sons Fred and Richard, and daughter Betty, together with Edna Mae and Chris Egemeier, had enjoyed a couple of days together in Bukavu, a beautiful lakeside city barely inside the eastern border of Zaire. After shopping for supplies, inspecting an exhibit and visiting friends, they were on their way back to Kama.

As usual, Sam was driving the four-ton Chevrolet truck, with Marie and Edna Mae beside him in the cab. The others, including a couple of Africans, sat or stood in the back of the truck. The load consisted largely of drums of kerosene and gasoline, but also contained food, building supplies and tools.

After safely traversing the mountains east of Bukavu, the travelers rode through rolling jungle country. About halfway down a hill, Sam was shifting into a lower gear when the rear axle snapped and the truck began to gather speed. Sam tried the emergency brake, but it failed to work. He knew what awaited them below—a sharp curve and then the bridge. Everybody hung on and prayed.

Just then the housing broke, and the axle dragged the ground—serving to brake the truck. Thus, Sam was able to maneuver the vehicle into a wide spot off the side of the road just before reaching the curve and the bridge.

Everybody heaved a sigh of relief and praised the Lord, but they still faced a dilemma. The truck was out of service. They were 50 miles from Bukavu and nearly 200 miles from Kama. Remembering that they had seen a placer mine on a hillside a short distance away, Vinton and Egemeier set off by foot to get help. The others stayed by the truck.

A walk of about a mile and a half brought them to the mine, where they found a cottage housing a lone Belgian supervisor. He immediately agreed to help. The three men went back to the truck in a Landrover, picked up the ladies and drove to a Norwegian Protestant Mission about ten miles away. Fred Vinton and his two helpers remained to guard the truck. Fred, an excellent mechanic, had already started dismantling the rear axle assembly and had prepared a list of replacement parts.

Cordially received by Rev. and Mrs. Lindstadt, Norwegian missionaries, the Vintons and Egemeiers refreshed themselves, enjoyed a table spread before them with good things to eat, and then accepted an invitation to spend the night. Upon hearing of their problem, Lindstadt prepared his Ford pickup truck to take his guests to Kama the next morning—true to the "Code of the Congo": help anyone in trouble.

On the way to Kama, Lindstadt drove and the wives shared the front seat. Sam and Chris, with the inevitable "boy chauffeur" or assistant, and the others crouched in the back. Something new about Sam Vinton came to light. He cannot ride in the back of a vehicle. No sooner had they gone a few miles than Baba Vi became violently ill. Edna Mae Egemeier finally came back and exchanged seats with Sam.

Making fairly good time, the truck reached within 50 miles of Kama, when once again came the ominous *crack*. Sure enough, the rear axle of the pickup had snapped, and the truck was grounded. Lindstadt, a big heavy man with slow and deliberate movements, left the driver's seat, came around to inspect the damage, shook his head and said, with his quaint Norwegian accent, "It's a hard *yob* to get to Kama!"

Within an hour, they resumed their journey. Paul Navara, a young Swiss agriculturist, who was helping with the rice plant near Kama, came by in his old beat-up pickup (often jokingly called "the wheelbarrow"). Though loaded with sacks of potatoes, the truck still had room enough for everyone to squeeze in, some on top of the sacks. Sam had arranged to send a mechanic and some parts back to Lindstadt. This time they made Kama without incident, all agreeing "it's a hard *yob* to get to Kama."

Of nine round trips missionary colleague Bill Bunch made with Sam Vinton from Kama to Bukavu (1961-63), one incident stood out vividly in his mind. On a return trip from Bukavu, after Bunch had signed a contract with the National Government to teach in their Christian schools, they found construction workers rebuilding a fairly large bridge just outside of Bukavu.

Stopped by the workmen, the missionaries explained where they were going. Sometimes the workmen would not be paid for months at a time, so now they wanted money before they would allow the travelers to cross the bridge. As they discussed the situation, the foreman came up and greeted Vinton warmly.

"This is our Baba, our father," he said to his workers. "He is not required to pay anything."

An argument ensued, and the workmen became so infuriated they started throwing planks off the bridge into the river. The foreman persisted.

"Baba Vi, don't you pay them a remea (about a penny in U.S. money)," he shouted. "Let them kill you first, but don't you dare pay! You are our father and you have the right to cross the bridge for nothing."

At the suggestion of Bill Bunch, Vinton promised to pay the workers. Then, after the two missionaries had crossed the bridge, Sam got out of the car, took out $20.00 in African money and gave half to the workmen, half to the foreman.

"I am not required to pay you anything," he reminded the workers. "Your foreman is authority. You are to obey him. But I realize you have not been paid in a long time, and you need something to eat."

Another time, on the trip from Kama to Bukavu, torrential rains had preceded them. Henry Sonneveldt (visiting at the time), Bill Bunch and Sam Vinton traveled in a two-door car—always a precarious experience on African roads without a four-wheel drive.

One area, between two rivers, was completely flooded.

By midnight moonlight, they found a raft, pushed the car onto the raft and enlisted helpers to push the raft down the middle of the road. Suddenly, the raft slipped off the road and Bill Bunch fell into a ditch up over his head. Incongruously, loud laughter punctuated the midnight scene. Finally, the raft was pushed back onto the road and with its precious cargo traveled more than a mile and a half before reaching drier ground. Then they drove the car off the handmade raft and continued on to Bukavu.

In June 1964—during the Simba uprisings—Bill and Mary Bunch were teaching at Kakumbu with other missionaries (from the Berean Mission). Shortwave radio informed them that the rebels were coming closer and closer. The missionaries gave their examinations early and closed the school five days ahead of schedule, then sent the students home. Sam Vinton, aware of the danger, came from Kama to rescue the students and fellow missionaries and take them to Bukavu.

On the frightening trip, Baba Vi proved to be a stabilizing influence as the car ran out of gas and people along the way were afraid of them. At one roadblock, the missionary entourage was completely surrounded by men—with spears, bows and arrows—deathly afraid, thinking the rebel forces had come. Vinton had all the car lights turned on, so the people could see who they were. Then he negotiated safe passage of the missionary caravan, convincing them they meant no harm.

Nine days after the rescue, the rebels entered Kakumbu and killed nine villagers.

July 4, 1967, the American Consul in Bukavu had a fourth of July celebration, although America's Independence Day didn't mean all that much to the Africans. The missionaries were all invited, Sam Vinton, Jr., Mama Vi and all the other missionaries went, except for one; Baba Vi was "down country" at Kama.

The evening got underway with a short program by the missionary children, which included "America, the Beautiful" and an acrostic, which had been written for the occasion. The children did well and everyone, including the VIP Africans and VIP diplomats from other countries, enjoyed it immensely.

Then, it was time for those who knew them to join in the singing of various American folk songs. All went well until the leader announced that the next one would be "Joshua Fit the Battle of Jericho." He began some lively chords on his guitar and by the time it was half through he was "swinging" it so much that the missionaries began feeling very much out of place.

A typical American picnic dinner was served with Cokes for the missionaries and beer for the guests who desired it. Some of them

58

were very unhappy because there was no hard liquor served. In order to keep in their good graces the Consul reluctantly brought it out. The last thing he wanted to do was to offend the Congolese authorities. To them, an important part of being a VIP was heavy drinking.

The evening closed with the showing of an interesting film. Everyone felt they had had a good time, in spite of differences of opinion in some areas of drink and entertainment. Mama Vi had enjoyed the evening; too bad Baba Vi had had to miss it!

Early the next morning, everyone was hearing strange noises. It sounded like the noise of fire-crackers but who would have those in Zaire?

"BANG! BANG! BANG!" Missionaries and Consulate Staff members (and no doubt many Africans) jumped out of their beds, all thinking the same thoughts, *"Those are rifle shots!"*

Soon, Sam, Jr. was running from door to door. "The Consul just called. He doesn't know what is happening but *a battle is taking place.* He says everyone is to stay in their houses until further notice."

Soon word came that a large group of mercenaries and Katangese soldiers had come in the night. They had taken over the soldiers' barracks and were trying to take over the whole city.

The shooting continued all day with some shots coming frighteningly close to various missionaries. At a lull in the fighting, some of them had to be rescued out of precarious places. Mama Vi, at the Guest House, desperately wished that Baba Vi were in Bukavu with her.

Finally, the Consul was able to make arrangements with the rebel forces to evacuate all Americans, and anyone else who wished to go. Twenty-seven carloads of people lined up at the Guest House at 2:00 P.M. Everyone waited for the signal to leave. That is, everyone but Mama Vi and their friends, the Cassells. They decided to stay; maybe Baba Vi could get up to Bukavu.

The Consul led the long line of cars down one of the main streets and on to the Ruzizi river. The rebels had agreed to cease firing until the convoy passed. Everyone breathed a sigh of relief upon arriving at the bridge and finding, indeed, no soldiers there.

"Whew-w-w-w!" whistled a number of missionaries as they crossed the bridge and started up the hill on the Rwanda side of the Ruzizi.

But — WAIT! The hill on the Rwanda side was covered with Rwandese soldiers, running down toward the cars. In a moment, they opened fire on the caravan!

To everyone's amazement, the Consul, at the lead, stopped his Land Rover and got out in full view, waving his hands in a signal of peace to the approaching, firing soldiers. At the same time, his wife was waving to the evacuees' cars to quickly pass on up the hill. Most missionaries had not witnessed such courage before!

The shooting stopped. The caravan passed safely on to a safe stopping place where everyone pulled off on the shoulder of the road. The Consul checked to see if there had been any casualties. Sam, Jr., who had been driving a VW bug, came running back to Ernie Green's car, shouting, "Ernie, they shot at me! One shot landed right in front of the 'bug' and another right behind it!"

"Everything is O.K.," the Consul said. Then, he explained, "Those Rwandese soldiers knew white mercenaries are attacking Bukavu. They thought we were the mercenaries, coming over to attack Rwanda. Drive on to the airstrip and await further instructions."

The next morning, after sleeping in cars or on the hangar floor, the missionaries and Consulate staff had a sorrowful experience. The women with children, plus the single ladies, were all flown out by a U.S. C-123 to Kigali. The husbands and wives with no children there and the men whose wives and children had been flown out, or who were single, were allowed to stay around the airport or drive on to a conference ground in Rwanda. The separation was difficult, even for the Consulate staff.

And what of Mama Vi back in Bukavu? Or Baba Vi at Kama? Mama Vi and her friends had a very frightening time. For some reason, the rebels suddenly left the city, leaving it in the hands of the regular Congolese Army. They decided to take "revenge" on any white people left in the city. Pulling up at the house right behind the Guest House, they ordered the white man to give them all his money. He did so but they believed he had more. When he insisted that he didn't have, they ordered the whole family outdoors and shot him right in front of his wife and children! Mama Vi and Cassells heard the commotion, the shots and the screaming of the wife and children.

After doing what they could for the family, they took council and decided they had better try to get out of Bukavu, after all. Baba Vi would have to try to get out of Congo alone. Thankfully, each one made it out and Baba and Mama Vi were re-united again in Kampala.

Mrs. (Marie) Vinton with

Sam and Marie Vinton   Kama Girls's School "Open Air" Sewing Class

Baba Vi (Sam Vinton) and Wami Medicine Men

Pastor Enoke Paul greets soldiers

Kama Literature Center

Bukavu Center

Zairian youngsters welcome missionaries to their village

Baba Vi visits with lepers

Mr. Vinton in Medical Unit

Mr. Vinton expounds the Word

Kama Station

Andre Assumani,
Pastor of Kama Church

Church service in Kama

Albert Mukula,
Director of Bible Schools

Yakobo Bitingo, starting on Evangelistic Trip

CHAPTER 8

Oasis in the Jungle

In a one-square-mile section of Kivu province lies Kama—one of the most indescribably beautiful and tragically needy areas of the world.

"This whole country turns from the hub of Kama mission," declares Sam Vinton. "If they run out of anything, they come to Kama. If something needs welding, they come to Kama. If someone needs healing, they come to Kama." And a visitor to the area certainly could not argue the point. Even the weather is predictable enough to allow guests their choice of visiting times.

Kama has four seasons: the big rains; the small rains; the long dry season; the short dry season. Throw in an occasional earthquake and you have plenty of variety. Usually the tremors are mild, though sometimes a major shock brings terror to the area.

All around the beautiful compound, as if in an entirely different world, lies the village of Kama—land of the great Warega tribe, with their ruling chiefs, brave hunters, skilful blacksmiths, powerful Bwamis in majestic dress, who dance and sing as they call upon their ancestral spirits . . . .

. . . blacksmiths, who forge sharp hunting knives, beautiful and strong hunting spears, axes to fell the giant trees and split firewood, with their talking drums that send messages by code from village to village during the night hours . . .

. . . industrious farmers, who each year clear and plant rice fields, banana patches, and cultivate peanuts and corn . . .

. . . brave hunters to track down and kill (with spears) the elephants, buffalo, wild pigs and antelopes, to provide meat for the family . . . :

. . . of dense rain forests, hot tropical sun, cool evenings and comfortable nights; of unpredictable tropical storms; the rumble of thunder, the flashes of lightning, the pouring rain—all joining in an ear-splitting crescendo.

By 5:30 in the morning, the jungle comes alive with the sound of music—a chorus of nature featuring birds, insects, animals, roosters,

61

goats and even a stray kitten or two. Add to that the voices of security guards—armed nationals—around the guest house, and you have a maelstrom of noises that proves a bit unnerving to the visiting writer.

Within an hour, other human voices—some crying pitifully—can be heard not many yards away as mothers with their children, plus a few men and children, begin to line up for medical attention at the dispensary. They know Sam Vinton will be there by 7:00 o'clock with a sympathetic hand of help.

Chickens noisily peck at the finely manicured lawns, which are criss-crossed with gravel footpaths. Stately palm trees, one for each Vinton child and grandchild, have been planted and now flourish near their residence. Beautiful flowers line the paths, giving a pleasing taste of civilization in the most primitive surroundings.

Years ago, when the Vintons first came to the area, nothing but ordinary forest trees could be seen everywhere. Today, in addition to the beautiful palms, mahogany trees provide the best kind of lumber wood, some of which is exported to Bukavu and other areas. Also, oranges, tangerines, grapefruit, guava, lemon, avocado and papaya have been introduced to the region.

Kivu province, where the Vintons have labored all these years, is the third largest of nine provinces in the country. About one-fifth of Zaire's 24 million people live there. Kivu is bordered on the north by the "Mountains of the Moon," on the south by the Zaire river, on the west by a lush tropical forest and on the east by the Eastern Great Rift.

Volcanic mountains—some still active—abound in the Lake Kivu area. Bukavu, the provincial capital, overlooks the beautiful lake from its 5,000-foot elevation.

In Eastern Zaire live the Lega, who are divided into three administrative territories—Mwenga, Shabunda and Pangi. It is in the latter two that Grace Mission works, along with the Evangelization Society African Mission (ESAM).

Just three degrees south of the Equator, Kama enjoys a good climate and plenty of rainfall. But those benefits do not guarantee any kind of health or prosperity.

Because of multiple malaria deaths in the early years of missionary service in the Belgian Congo (now Zaire), such a divine call became known as a "short cut to heaven." But that terminology failed to take into account the God Who provided strength and promised, "Lo, I am with you always."

To many who sat in darkness for years, Kama is a lighthouse whose rays penetrated the hearts of forest villagers. Many similar lighthouses, patterned after the Kama church, are bringing people to Christ and the new life He provides.

Girls and women—the burden-bearers—walk majestically erect across the compound and through the village, carrying their pans of food or pails of water, or a dozen heavy pieces of firewood piled on a carrier, balanced perfectly atop their heads.

A tour of the Saturday morning outdoor market in the village, graciously escorted by Marie Vinton, proves an eye-opener. Located little more than one hundred yards from the mission station itself, about halfway to the nearby hospital, the market majors in variety.

Gathered around the merchants, mostly women, who display their products on the ground as they sit, are hundreds of villagers already on hand at the 7 o'clock hour. When a slight drizzle begins to fall, Mama Vi's well-trained houseboys quickly appear with umbrellas—and the tour continues.

Small whitened eggplants; manioc (looks much like the sweet potato); lenga lenga ("hog greens," similar in taste to spinach); small chickens—all are offered by the enterprising merchants.

Large, handmade wooden spoons—with beautiful designs burned into the handle—are available; also chili peppers, curry (manzame), dried and powdered, and used as seasoning; mangoes, and salt—sold in glasses of various sizes.

For packaging the items, large forest leaves are used. Dried fish and soap (locally made, from palm oil and lye) are seen in abundance. Fried cakes are not too appetizing in appearance, but Mama Vi says they are quite tasty.

Thin rice gruel, plantain (large green bananas, good for cooking as a staple food—and for banana chips) add color and variety to the market "menu."

An outdoor "restaurant" is simply a small roped-off area with a makeshift leaf shelter, under which a few villagers already have begun to make use of some of the purchased items as their breakfast.

Several kinds of flour are featured—made from rice, manioc and cassava (the latter "tastes like rubber," Mama Vi says). In some areas the flour is mixed with corn to become more edible, and is soaked in a stream for two or three days. "Their code of ethics forbids stealing food while it is soaking!" she explains.

Then come the sundries: locks and keys, shoe polish, thread, mothballs, blades, batteries, hard candy, needles, thongs (sandals), nylon cord, used clothing. Mama Vi stops along the way to buy an occasional item, chatting cheerfully with her friends, always leaving them with warm smiles.

A few yards away, over in the tall grass, perhaps half a dozen men are busily engaged. "Butchering a goat," Mama Vi explains.

An occasional question is directed at the gracious missionary lady. "What do the earth tremors mean?" (Four minor shocks had occurred in recent days). "What's this we hear about an eclipse of the sun in 1980?" Marie Vinton takes advantage of the opportunities to apply Scripture to the dilemmas that bother the villagers.

Later in the morning, a parade of school children—honoring the guests—was held on the compound lawn. With rain as a delaying factor, ceremonies began an hour and a half late—at about 10:30 o'clock. A quickly formed "reviewing stand"—a long row of chairs in front of the guest house—included Sam and Marie Vinton, national church leaders, other missionaries and American guests.

Some 1200 students from three primary schools and two secondary schools, with their teachers, marched sharply in front of the official onlookers—led by four boys carrying "talking drums," made out of huge logs.

Boys and girls of all ages, saluting with hand across the heart, marched briskly by. Finally circling half the compound, the students stood in place as they sang their national anthem with obvious enthusiasm and respect.

A group of half a dozen girls walked up to the reviewing stand, then sang a welcome song especially composed for the occasion. The names of the American guests could be heard among the many strange words.

Then, in English—learned specifically for these ceremonies—a student says, "I want to be wise. Can anyone help me?" A second student responds in his broken English, "Proverbs 1:7, 'The fear of the Lord is the beginning of wisdom.' "

Sam and Marie Vinton glow with pride. Their charges have been trained well.

When a student asks about the Word of God, one of the young men replies, "In the beginning was the Word."

Still another young man comes forward with his question, "I want to be saved. What can I do? Is there anyone to help me?" A student appears immediately with his response, "Yes, I can help you. 'Neither is there salvation in any other name.' "

In typical African offbeat rhythm, with broken English, the students sing "Nothing But the Blood of Jesus," an exciting moment in the course of the ceremonies—calling to mind the oneness in Christ enjoyed by men and women, boys and girls of all nationalities.

Then the questions and answers resume. "How does God love us? Do you think God loves us? Is there anyone to answer?" A young man quickly appears to reply. "Yes. John 3:16 says, 'For God so loved the world that He gave His only begotten Son, that whosoever believeth in Him should not perish but have everlasting life.' "

One final question comes from a student, "I want to believe; can you help me?" The response, "Ecclesiastes 12:1, 'Remember now thy creator.' "

After a group of young men sing—again in broken English—

64

"There's a Welcome Here," a gymnastic performance features a half dozen boys hurling themselves through hoops held vertically. Then two fellows on their backs help other athletes perform double somersaults by propelling them forward through the air.

Then comes fun time, for the students and the reviewers as well, as two boys stand about six feet apart, each with the end of a string in his mouth—object: to chew until one or the other reaches a piece of candy tied in the middle.

After that exciting performance, two other young men are blindfolded, handed spoons and placed beside a chair containing a bowl of rice. Their object is to feed each other until the rice is all gone. Very little of the food actually reaches either mouth, until one of the fellows decides it's easier to feed himself.

Turning to a more serious side, the parade organizers call on Henry Sonneveldt, mission board president emeritus, for a few remarks.

"We appreciate your testimony for the Lord," the mission executive begins. "I know that the leadership of the church in this area is going to come out of you young people. Education is very, very important, but knowing the Lord Jesus Christ as personal Saviour is most important of all. Even you children can make a decision for the Lord.

"Remember that as you study your lessons in school, you should also study the Word of God. Be proud of your country and be proud of your God. As you apply yourself to education and to service for the Lord, you will make a great country out of Zaire. I return to America greatly encouraged by what I have seen and heard here today."

An impartial observer would have to agree. Missionary influence in the Kama area of Zaire, quite obviously, has made a difference. Some might consider it only scratching the surface, but even the most pessimistic would have to call it a mighty deep scratch.

Problems still exist, of course—many of them—and one critical lack is that of food, the shortage of which leads to considerable thievery. Some villagers steal from each other's gardens. Total population in the village is only about 700, but add an equal number of guests or visitors at a given time and you have a serious situation with regard to food supplies.

Uprisings and rebellion set back the momentum and progress of Kama perhaps 10 years, Sam Vinton believes. But new strides are being made today, and the veteran missionary is hopeful a growing band of young missionaries will emerge to facilitate that growth.

When the occasion demands, Baba Vi can be both persistent and insistent. An administration commission came to Kama one day and sought to ban the use of Christian songs on the loudspeaker.

"I'll comply when I get orders from the president of our church in

Kinshasa," Vinton told the startled officials.

Always on the lookout for helpful equipment that will facilitate the missionaries' work, the Vintons utilize the services of travelers coming and going to bring in new items—whether other missionaries on furlough or simply visiting mission officials. In that way, they obtained a light plant years earlier, plus photographic equipment for one of the Vinton-trained nationals.

One can hardly be with the Vintons—either or both—for five minutes without interruption by nationals—people in need. And with their open door policy, Sam and Marie always make themselves available to respond.

Three eggs, a token of love and friendship, came to Mama Vi one afternoon from a traveling African who brought the gift from someone in a nearby village simply wanting to express appreciation.

As we continue our interview with Sam Vinton, a young man drops by the veranda to report the illness of Pastor Asumani. Baba Vi leaves immediately for the dispensary to obtain medicine for the sick man.

Mama Vi points to a man working in the nearby garden. "He's from Kisangani, and he has a serious skin problem. That's how he earns his medicine."

A villager brings in his wife who is suffering with a gall bladder problem. Sam Vinton wastes no time in taking her to the dispensary for treatment.

That kind of activity characterizes the daily life of the Vintons—always available for people in need, *their* people.

One afternoon the big man himself, Chief Funga Funga, ruler over 41 villages, asks for an audience with Baba Vi and Sonneveldt. They assume he will be asking for help of some kind.

"I came just to thank you and Grace Mission for sending Baba and Mama Vi and the other missionaries to Zaire," the chief tells his surprised listeners. "With your permission, I would like to use them as technical advisers as we seek to rebuild our country."

Part of that rebuilding program involves oil extraction from the stately palms, which is a thriving enterprise in the Kama area.

"We now have 21 oil extraction centers scattered throughout our villages," Sam Vinton says. "Most of them are set up and operated by church groups. These centers produce more than ten tons of palm oil every month. This is used in cooking, as shortening, and much of it is exported. Palm trees bear all year long and have a life span of 50 years."

When a United Nations patrol came to the Kama station during the time of rebellion, their members called the compound a "delightful oasis in the middle of the jungle." Visitors today recognize it as a place of unparalleled hospitality—the home of Baba

66

and Mama Vi, who welcome everyone with a comfortable chair and a cup of coffee or tea.

Kama area villagers call the mission the "home of missionaries who care"—enough to leave the comforts of their homes in the United States, travel over bad roads and dangerous bridges to come to our villages, hold Gospel meetings, teach the Word of God where once people worshiped idols, were in sin and darkness—now are saved and worshiping the living God.

"They bring us medicine, and many of us are living today because missionaries cared enough to come out. We go to Kama to have our babies—on planter sheets instead of on the earthen floor or on the ground. How nice to have a hot cup of coffee or tea after being in labor for several hours, to have Baba Vi come and check and assure us that everything is okay.

"Our children go there to get an education. Do you believe the 'Word of God is quick and powerful?' We at Kama do. Do you believe Romans 1:16 ('For I am not ashamed of the gospel of Christ; for it is the power of God unto salvation to everyone that believeth; to the Jew first, and also to the Greek.') We at Kama do."

Thanks to the Voice of America and other international radio news broadcasts, the Vintons and their colleagues are not cut off entirely from the rest of the world. They listen eagerly to the 10 p.m. news. They learned about the American hostages in Iran for example at the same time the rest of the world did.

Ambitious young people are not a rarity in the Kama area. On the day of departure for the American visitors, a handsome young African, Masudi Selemani-Wenda, 22, introduced himself in fairly distinct English. He expressed a deep desire to further his education in America, and promised to correspond with his new American friends.

One thing the nationals know for certain: if they want to work to further their education, to buy supplies for their studies, or for other good reasons, they have a friend and ally in Sam Vinton, who will find some way to *make* work if necessary so that the needs might be met.

A onetime assistant to the late Senator Everett Dirksen of Illinois, Robert W. Harms, later an executive with the Mennonite Central Committee, visited Kama a few years ago.

Writing in *The Christian Reader,* Harms pointed out that "at Kama you find the big brick church with the thatched roof. On some Sundays, as many as 1,700 people crowd in to hear the service. The local community built it and paid for it.

"There is no question of fusion of mission and church or fight over property rights. It was crystal clear from the beginning that the church belonged to the community, not to the missionaries."

Harms added, "Community development has long been a way of life at Kama. Sam Vinton made his principles clear from the beginning. There are no handouts. 'Nothing for nothing' goes the slogan. If you want something you must work. The second principle was equally clear: If the community does the work, it should reap the benefits."

As a home base for the mission activity, Kama is a strange study in contrasts. Right in the midst of the most primitive jungles in all of Zaire, standing like a beacon to guide the wayfarer, is what some have described as the most beautiful mission station in the world—home of the valorous Vintons for most of their lives.

Thus, the mission station at Kama has been recognized for its great contribution to the country of Zaire, to its people, to the whole cause of missions. One great factor in the success of the Kama program is the whole area of medicine. Such an extensive undertaking has proved itself over and over again.

CHAPTER 9

Medicine: Open Door to the Heart

Carrying a gun and spear, Mubule Paul stalked the steaming jungle, seeking to track down the wild chimpanzees who were making havoc of the muhoko garden. As chief hunter for the Kama region, Mubule could be counted on for the success of his assignments, and he walked stealthily toward his prey.

Suddenly, a long sharp spear zoomed toward the wary hunter. He sought to pull back, but the speeding weapon—misdirected by a fellow hunter—sliced his throat and anchored into his shoulder.

Nearby villagers, quickly recognizing the emergency, carried Mubule to the dispensary. Sam Vinton, alerted to the need, sutured to stop the bleeding and then sewed up his neck. Mama Vi, meanwhile, called for the small plane—piloted by Jack Spurlock—to come and fly him to the hospital in Bukavu for further emergency treatment.

Weathered in for 48 hours, Spurlock finally was able to make the hour-long flight from Bukavu to Kama and pick up his emergency patient. Saline and glucose solutions, given the wounded hunter by Baba Vi, helped to keep him steady.

At the Katana hospital not far from the Bukavu airport, doctors praised the emergency treatment already administered to Mubule Paul by the veteran Zaire missionary. Satisfied with what they saw, the physicians decided not to reopen the wound. Ten days later, they released Mubule and he was able to return to Kama, well on the road to recovery.

"Had we not been here," Baba Vi observed, "Mubule would have bled to death. So it's great to be at a place where you count for something.

"This kind of emergency might happen as often as a dozen times a month, so we're glad to be available for such things, as well as for the ordinary everyday physical needs of the people."

Except for the availability of medicines five air hours away in Nairobi, Kenya, Baba Vi and his capable coworkers could not respond to such emergencies. On one trip to that beautiful,

69

cosmopolitan city—crossroads for many African travelers—Vinton came back with many thousands of dollars worth of medicines. Spurlock and others have obtained supplies for Kama on numerous occasions.

Baba Vi's nurse and chief assistant, Maria Nzoloko, was once a student in the Kama schools. Suffering a serious skin disease, she would have died had she not come to the dispensary for treatment. An African healer had provided no help at all. Vinton immediately prescribed shots of Vitamin E, improving the condition perceptively and ten years later Maria is a picture of health—the mother of 3-year-old Salima, the smiling charmer whose glistening white teeth shine like a beacon through ebony black features and whose favorite resting place is in the lap of Baba Vi.

On this Monday morning, 75-80 patients have formed an irregular line beside the dispensary window. Pastor Kingumba Augustin reads to them from the Word of God, usually basing a few helpful and encouraging remarks on John 3:16 before praying earnestly for the mothers and their children, plus a few men and young people.

Soon, Baba Vi strides rapidly across the compound from his residence, right around the normal 7 o'clock opening time. His dispensary window is raised for the work of the clinic to begin.

Maria, busily engaged the whole time—with continuous assistance from Pastor Augustin—packages pills, measures out syrups and other medicines, at the same time listening to the animated conversation between Baba Vi and the patients.

Obviously loved and respected by his co-workers and also by the patients, Sam Vinton's handling of individual cases might seem autocratic at times—to the uninformed observer. To handle his daily schedule, Baba Vi must act quickly, must insist on the small minimal payment before treatment ("nothing for nothing") and must help the Africans protect themselves by not giving them more than one day's treatment at a time.

"The temptation is too great either to take all of the medicine at one time, thinking that a multiplied dosage will speed the healing, or to share the pills and other medicine with family or friends," Vinton explains.

Since some of the patients stand in line for several hours, mostly awaiting the normal opening time for the dispensary, national pastors have provided a makeshift but serviceable magazine rack for the children to help keep them occupied. Suitable stories and pictures hold the interest of waiting boys and girls easing the strain on concerned parents.

One woman approaches the window with a babe in arms, her twin securely fastened to the mother's back. Baba Vi quickly discerns the problem and the need, and Maria hands out a bottle of syrup to

70

destroy worms—a common problem with the Africans. Sensing the mother's need for help in giving the distasteful medicine to her children, Pastor Augustin remains close at hand and assists her in the unpleasant task.

A man appears at the window with an unusual request. He has come all the way from Bukavu—several days by foot and occasional truck—with a prescription from his doctor to obtain medicine for the man's mother. Baba Vi assures him he will see that the prescription goes with Jack Spurlock on the next plane back to Bukavu.

One by one they come, with a variety of ailments and needs. Leprosy, dysentery, malaria, anemia, hookworms, roundworms, scabies, abscesses to be dressed, teeth to be pulled, injections needed, hair to be cut so that ointment can be applied to inflamed scalps, drops for sore eyes and infected ears.

Childless couples often come to Baba Vi for infertility treatments, and the Kama dispensary has experienced success in 72 percent of such cases. Many nationals attribute magical powers to the skilled septuagenarian.

Dental needs occupy a large portion of Vinton's time. Tired of walking and working with a throbbing toothache, one African man came with his wife and children one day—after walking a day and a half, then crossing the Elela river in a dugout canoe to reach Kama.

While they waited for Baba Vi to arrive, Marie served them hot tea and pancakes—a treasured feast for the weary travelers. A quick extraction relieved the jolting pain, and the grateful family returned to their village the next day.

Often, relieved patients make special trips back to the mission station to express their thanks for the treatment given them, sometimes with gifts of appreciation that require great sacrifice on their part. Most Africans are very thoughtful in matters of this kind.

Baba Vi explains his philosophy of healing. "I believe God made the body. I believe He made it perfect. The machine can't run perfectly if there's some dirt in the gas. The body can't operate normally if there are worms in the stomach or malaria germs in the body.

"We try to remove the obstructions so the normal healing process can take place. I believe there are several ways we can help the body; i.e., iron for anemia, fortifying tonics and vitamins. Preventive measures—better drinking water, better housing, better food—are extremely important, too."

When Vinton is not to be available at the dispensary on a given morning because of safaris or other reasons, the village grapevine effectively communicates the news so that the ailing Africans are spared long walks and waits. Especially needy cases can come to Rich Nymeyer at the nearby "hospital"—whose almost bare rooms hardly qualify the place for the normal appellation.

"Our health centers are so located that no one has to walk more than five miles for treatment—in most cases," Vinton explains. Many want to come for special treatment at the Kama dispensary, of course, and that explains the early morning lineup that often reaches a hundred or more patients.

When a man arrives at the dispensary with carbuncles all over his body, Baba Vi sends him to the hospital for penicillin injections. He will have to go back two days later for more.

One of Vinton's medical assistants, standing outside the window alongside the pastor as sort of an "intermediary," whispers a special word to the elderly missionary. When all of the other patients have left, he wants to come and have a tooth pulled—he values his privacy!

A man with an infected incision appears for treatment. Baba Vi gives him an antibiotic. An Army chaplain, living in one of the rooms for Bible school students, comes to receive treatment for an ear running with pus. An antibiotic and ascorbic acid are prescribed.

Always maintaining a positive, cheerful attitude, regardless of the severity of the cases, Vinton finds time as he talks with his patients to tease his young assistant, Maria, about her new hairdo. A beautiful young mother in her own right, the shy medical assistant smiles and ducks her head. A dozen or so prongs stick straight out of her hair, with marble-size cloth balls atop each prong. Even that strange sight does not mar her natural beauty.

The makeshift clinic, or dispensary, or pharmacy—as it has been variously called—might bring grey hairs to distinguished officials of the American Medical Association, but the fact remains that it works, as evidenced by tens of thousands who bear testimony to healing as a result of their treatment at Kama.

The two-room (both extremely small) clinic barely has room for Vinton and Maria to dispense their medicines, plus a small supply room containing shelves that hold bottles and other containers of all sizes. Fortunately, both Baba Vi and Maria know just where to put their hands on any particular medicine or pill when necessary.

Vinton laughs when an observer notes the rigid daily routine he sets for himself, involving him with patients bearing diseases and ailments of all kinds.

"I have the easiest job in the world," he says. "Others do everything for me. These nationals appreciate responsibility, and some have been with me for 15 or 20 years." None of this would be possible, of course, without the skill and leadership of Sam Vinton.

Vitamins and cough medicines are used freely, so they are prepared for handing out well in advance. "We buy 10,000 empty bottles at a time," Vinton explains. "And we ask the patients to bring them back after use, or pay for them. That helps to keep us well supplied."

72

Maria mixes camphorated oil to put on the chests of children. "We always buy high potency medicines and dilute them," Baba Vi says. "In that way we save space and expense."

Tuberculosis patients must pay for eight weeks of treatment right at the start. "We would have 500 TB patients lined up if the treatment were free," Vinton explains. "And of course there's no way we can handle that many with our limited staff and facilities."

A young man comes with an eye swollen shut; another has a strep throat. Appropriate antibiotics and penicillin are prescribed. Most of the shots are actually given at the hospital, where Dr. Rich Nymeyer, a chiropractor with training at the School of Tropical Medicine in Antwerp, Belgium, and two government medical workers hold forth.

A crude, hard, wooden "examining table" occupies the center of one otherwise bare small room in the brick building—with galvanized metal roof—that serves as a hospital. Nymeyer is examining a man with a low back problem. He feels the patient's back and stomach.

"The people here eat too many carbohydrates," Nymeyer explains. "The major problem is nutrition. I try to tell them they can't build huts with mud alone—they must have sticks and leaves as well, and in the same way they can't build their bodies by eating carbohydrates alone. A full and complete diet is needed.

"Until the staple crops come in—peanuts, rice, manioc—they suffer from seasonal hunger. They haven't learned to store things for the off season, but they are learning slowly. We must change their whole cycle, their lifestyle: where they plant, and when.

"And the problem is magnified by the lack of good communication. Unlike America, word-of-mouth is the major means of spreading the word about nutrition here in Zaire."

When patients must stay overnight at the hospital, for one or more nights, members of their family are accommodated in mission-furnished mud huts adjacent to the hospital and they are given food for their stay.

Incongruity seems to be a way of life in Zaire. Zooming by the small hospital buildings, a young man on a Yamaha 100 motorbike attracts considerable attention from the villagers—just as the football (soccer) game out in the jungle had seemed wildly incongruous, though reassuringly familiar to American visitors, who needed that brief reorientation to life outside the jungle.

Kyanga Louis, one of the male nurses at the hospital, received Christ as Saviour at a Youth for Christ meeting in the Kama area. Like many other nationals, he is an invaluable part of the healing team under Sam Vinton's supervision.

Kama's first dispensary was built in 1932 after the Vintons returned from Belgium with a supply of medicines.

"I called the elders and chiefs together," Vinton explains, "and told them I had many medicines and a diploma, but no building in which to work. Then I asked them, 'Are you willing to put up a building—and furnish free labor?' ''

The church and village leaders held a three-day powwow to consider the matter. Finally, they agreed to the terms, and Baba Vi promised to supply doors, windows and other things the village could not provide.

"Our whole philosophy," Vinton explains, "is to train them in doing—to see that they do it right."

Two times in the subsequent five decades, the people had to rally together and rebuild the dispensary when rebels with a scorched-earth policy leveled the building.

"There are many ways to reach people," Baba Vi says. "The old way was to expect them to come in for treatment. The new way is to go out where they are in the villages. Because we believe preventive medicine is very important, we give them malaria pills once a week.

"On our safaris, we try to get to every village within a 50-mile radius at least once a month. We have 14 health centers—with about five villages to each center."

Down through the years, Sam and Marie Vinton have had to break down several long-standing traditions. One of these held that if a man comes near a woman in pregnancy, both the mother and the baby will die. Marie worked with the women in labor, and Sam helped. When they saved one African mother and her baby by a manual extraction, a committee of 25 mothers came to the Vintons one day.

"We knew God would help you," they said. "We want you to take care of all our babies. But you know our husbands won't let us come in."

So now the Vintons take expectant mothers to the hospital for delivery (after the mothers have surreptitiously appeared at the Vinton door or window and indicated the need). Previously, delivery had taken place out in the bush away from everything and everybody.

"You can follow the transforming power of the Gospel in every part of their lives," Vinton says.

Another long-held tradition was the circumcision ceremony. Young men didn't really belong to the tribe until they were circumcised. After long rituals, ceremonial dances and singing, the rite would take place and often infection would set in. Some of the children would die. One day, the chiefs asked Vinton to take care of all circumcision.

"I will," Baba Vi agreed, "but here's the way we will do it." Thereafter, the boys would be taken to a colony about one mile from Kama, accompanied by several pastors who taught them Gospel songs and Scripture verses. Then the actual circumcision would be performed at the hospital.

"We still take them through part of their traditional ceremony," Vinton explains, "so they can again become full-fledged members of their tribe. Changes do take place out here, slowly but surely."

One of those changes has been a dramatic turnabout in the number of childless couples. When the problem first became known to the Vintons, they wrote many authorities on the subject of infertility and obtained a large quantity of material. Then they worked with one couple for eight or nine months, testing the program.

"A couple of months later, the wife was pregnant," Vinton said. "Both are now working in Bukavu and taking theological training."

Sometimes both husband and wife need to be treated. "God has helped us save at least 500 couples from divorce or polygamy," Baba Vi added.

The Vintons are happy, too, that they were able to take 52 families from the leper settlement last year—arrested cases—and return them to their villages. Such medical dividends serve only to enhance their joy at lives changed spiritually.

Marie Vinton, in addition to her fine work with measles and whooping cough patients, majors in prenatal, maternal and postnatal care for mothers and their offspring. During the first ten months of 1979, 188 babies were born in the Kama hospital, and each mother was presented garments for their infants as gifts from caring women in the United States.

Some mothers have walked 20 miles for this kind of care. One mother came a total of 75 miles to receive Mama Vi's loving attention; another, 55 miles.

A one-year report of medical accomplishments at Kama gives some idea of the scope of the work. Number of new cases treated: 37,756; consultations: 111,033; enrolled in prenatal clinics: 1,222; prenatal consultations: 14,196; enrolled in baby clinics (under five): 1,787.

Number of lepers in settlement: 472; health centers: 13; villages reached through these centers: 51; miles traveled: 5,000; patients transported from outlying villages to Kama: 1,163; patients discharged from Kama: 901; members of staff (nationals): 14; members of staff (medical missionaries): 1; members of staff (educational): 1. Richard Nymeyer arrived a few months after this report was made, increasing the medical missionaries to two.

"Kama is the only hope for thousands in this area who need medical care," the Vintons say. "So we must not let them down but rather increase our efforts to meet their needs."

Occasional short-time visits from outsiders help to augment the medical program significantly.

"The year 1975, for example, closed with an unexpected visit from our friend Dr. Kawkiwictz of Bukavu who ran a clinic here at Kama medical center for special cases," Baba Vi reported.

"Dr. Rene Ledieu from Brussels, Belgium came with him and went on a weekend safari with our mobile team. Such visits are not only important and helpful from the medical point of view, but they really help in developing good public relations."

At the risk of repetition, Sam Vinton likes to emphasize the convenience aspect of the present medical setup.

"Instead of waiting for the sick to walk hours or even days to the Kama medical center, with the hot tropical sun beating down on them, and often arriving too late, our team meets the needs of the people in their home villages—a tremendous saving.

"The number of our hospital patient days at Kama has been cut from more than 2,700 to less than 900—or 1,800 days per month saved for extra work in their fields producing food instead of spending them in the hospital."

Vinton added, "Health centers are built and cared for by the local people, who also provide food and accommodations for the team at no cost to us."

Though the medical work necessarily remains on a much smaller scale than the Vintons would like, still they are making important strides in delivering health care to people who would otherwise be deprived of any kind of relief and would suffer until death overtook them.

One specialized branch of this work—that among the lepers—takes place about four miles from the Kama station. It is a dramatic ministry that reaches into the lives of thousands of people and shows the remarkable staying power of the human spirit, especially when the people involved are exercising a living faith.

CHAPTER 10

Life in the Leper Settlement

It was Sunday morning at the Kama station, around 8:30 o'clock. As on many another weekend, the big Ford F600 pickup truck was parked near the Vinton residence—ready to load its passengers.

Destination: the leper settlement some four miles away, which meant a half-hour journey on the treacherous roads that had lacked any kind of maintenance for ten years since the rebellion.

Sam Vinton took his usual place behind the wheel, with the "highway superintendent," Madou, beside him for direction and gear shifting. Henry Sonneveldt occupied the other seat in the cab.

Behind them, in the back of the truck, sat Marie Vinton and her American guest—this writer—in comfortable chairs, while wooden benches held members of the team plus several children who made the trip to visit relatives enroute or at the settlement.

In true Mama Vi fashion, she shared small dabs of Avon cream with the girls and women near her, fascinating them with the fragrance emanating from the lotion. The children smiled gleefully as they displayed their prized possession.

As on all such safaris, whether short or long, the loudspeaker rang out the good news of the Gospel in song. Excited villagers along the way, especially the children, ran toward the truck to greet the travelers, then raced alongside the vehicle shouting, "Baba Vi! Baba Vi!" When they sighted Mama Vi in the rear of the truck, they added her name to the warm greeting.

On hand at the compound to greet the visitors some 30 minutes later, Pastor Shindano Kilongo escorted them into the nearby village church—a part of the leper settlement—to begin the service at about 9:10 a.m. As with most such special occasions, the time of the service depended on the time of arrival of the visiting participants.

While being escorted to comfortable chairs on the platform, the guests heard the exciting songs of the church as presented by various groups of nationals. Again, in typical African fashion, the singing and swaying added a dramatic touch to the musical interlude, for the colorful singers—in most cases—followed tradition by decreasing in

77

volume perceptibly near the end of the song and ending in a near-whisper as they slowly descended to their seats.

The burned brick structure, with bamboo windows and swamp-leaf roofs, overflowed its capacity, and the doorways were jammed with would-be worshippers, while others peeked through the bamboo-slit windows.

"Singing is the best possible therapy for these people," Vinton said. "In earlier years, they sang praises to idols, to spirits—it was evil and satanic. Today all they know is our Gospel songs.

"They have a wonderful spirit of helping one another. Some who are in bad condition help others who are worse. Some carry water and firewood for others."

Early in the service, Pastor Kilongo calls on an old favorite of the lepers, Mama Vi, for a word of greeting to her friends. She never disappoints them.

"We were here two weeks ago," Marie begins. "Are you tired of seeing us?" A loud chorus of "No!" comes from the 200-plus worshipers.

"I am not tired of coming here, either," Mama Vi continues, smiling. "Our heart's cry is that we would like to come out more often, but we are so busy. It is just not possible for me to walk that far any more.

"The truck is out for the weekend all the time, so I can't come. Even though we don't see each other often, we still love each other. We are one by the Word of God. Isn't that true?"

A loud chorus of agreement echoes through the crowd, and an American visitor can see and feel the deep love and respect these people have for both Sam and Marie Vinton. The nationals strain to be sure no word is missed.

"I am not a preacher," Mama Vi reminds them. "I am one who helps to bring you food, and we don't bring raw food to you. We bring cooked food. What do you do with food? You eat it. Now, let's feed on the Word of God together.

"If you just look at the food, will it help you?" With smiles, they shake their heads. "You don't take that food and rub it on your stomach." (Loud laughter rings out.) "You put it in your mouths and stomachs.

"Is there anyone here without a box (stomach) down here (pointing)?" (Again, the "No" resounded.) "Baba Vi has a small box (loud laughter, knowing that their good friend never seems to eat very much). Now I want you to open up your ears and hear."

Marie Vinton then reads Paul's prayer for the church at Ephesus: "For this cause I bow my knees unto the Father of our Lord Jesus Christ, Of whom the whole family in heaven and earth is named, That he would grant you, according to the riches of his glory, to be strengthened with might by his Spirit in the inner man;

"That Christ may dwell in your hearts by faith; that ye, being rooted and grounded in love, May be able to comprehend, with all saints, what is the breadth, and length, and depth, and height, And to know the love of Christ, which passeth knowledge, that ye might be filled with all the fullness of God.

"Now unto him who is able to do exceedingly abundantly above all that we ask or think, according to the power that worketh in us, Unto him be glory in the church by Christ Jesus throughout all ages, world without end. Amen" (Ephesians 3:14-21).

Her eager audience listens attentively. Visitors marvel at the obvious impact of familiar Scriptural truths upon a totally different culture from their own.

"Are the bricks the church?" Marie asks. ("No!" they respond in unison.) "We are the church—you and I," she reminds them.

Articulate and forceful, Mama Vi knows how to speak the language of her African listeners, both dialectically and practically.

"This ground (pointing) is on the outside," she continues. "My breath is on the inside. So is Christ on the inside.

"Did you ever see a person take a chunk of elephant meat and try to swallow it? No, it would kill him. In the same way, we must take the Word of God in small pieces and feed on it."

Mama Vi has communicated well with her audience. And they are with her all the way, applauding her with hearty *Amens* and smiling broadly as she returns to her seat.

Pastor Kilongo then welcomes Henry Sonneveldt back to the church after a year's absence. It is obvious that the undershepherd and his flock are pleased at the visit of their American guest.

The articulate mission executive gains their attention and laughter by observing, "It seems like the women sing more than the men." That observation had not escaped this writer, who wondered about the disproportion. Then Sonneveldt becomes more serious.

"In the time since I was with you last year, I have had many good experiences, but one sad one." (Baba Vi interprets forcefully and with animation.) "Nine months ago, my dear wife—whom I loved very much and was married to for 45 years—died." (Murmurs of sympathy rise through the audience.)

"It is hard to be separated, but it is wonderful to know she is with the Lord. Almost 50 years ago, she received the Lord Jesus Christ as her personal Saviour. Almost 60 years ago, I did the same thing." Sonneveldt had learned years earlier that African audiences want and expect to hear personal information about the families of their speakers.

He continues, "I wonder if everyone in this service has made his or her decision for the Lord Jesus Christ. The Bible tells us we have

79

all sinned and come short of the glory of God. God sent His Son to die on the cross for our sins, so that we might have everlasting life.

"Jesus Christ said, 'I am the way, the truth and the life. No man cometh unto the Father but by me.' The Bible tells us Christ was crucified and rose again. If we believe that, the Bible promises, we will have everlasting life."

Quietly, eagerly, the people seem to take in every word. And you can tell that they wait as expectantly for Baba Vi.

Sam Vinton begins his message with a reference to the earth tremors that remain on the minds of many. As he speaks, a young mother on the front row strains to hear every word, while her baby feeds contentedly at her breast.

"God is longsuffering," Baba Vi says, "and He gives us His warnings. God's Word tells us, in Romans 15:17,18, 'I have, therefore, that of which I may glory through Jesus Christ in those things which pertain to God.

" 'For I will not dare to speak of any of those things which Christ hath not wrought by me, to make the Gentiles obedient, by word and deed.' "

Vinton then asks the crowd to pray for the visiting writer as he works on his book about the Kama ministry. Hundreds of Africans thus play a vital part in the preparation of this book by their prayers.

Ushers, mostly women, carry long sticks or poles with baskets on the end. While they perform their duties, they sing right along with the audience, swinging and swaying with the rhythm of their offbeat songs. At the end of the regular morning offering comes a special heart-rending presentation to the American guests.

One by one, some members of the congregation come to the platform and place an egg—a highly valued food for them—on an offering plate to be given to the visitors as a token of love and appreciation. More than a dozen eggs are given in this way.

Generosity and gratitude seem to characterize the African believers wherever we go. Their example will not soon be forgotten.

All is quiet in the audience except for an occasional crying baby. Mothers usually walk out quickly with their crying infants, for there seems to be a low level of tolerance for noisy children in African audiences.

Pastor Kilongo spends a few minutes expressing warm appreciation for his visitors. Then he addresses them directly, "You have chairs to sit in; you have some food (eggs). Now we are going to sing and talk some more about the Word of the Lord."

Half a dozen singing groups, one following the other without interruption, add to the worship of the morning with their enthusiastic vocal renditions. No instruments, only home-made rattles, add to the rhythm of the music.

Extemporaneous messages in song mark the creative presentation, strangely non-poetic though nonetheless effective. "These people who are suffering today without Christ will suffer worse in the life to come. Wherever You lead me, Lord, I want to go with you. The world is trying to hold me back, but I want to follow You."

A third group of singers, equally rhythmic with their beautiful harmony proclaim: "God is love. The love of God is shining in my heart now. In his love, Jesus is waiting for you. Without Him you would be lost."

Songbooks are nowhere to be seen. The people sing from their hearts, and their love for the One about Whom they sing is evident. Through all of the proceedings, an obviously delighted Sam Vinton beams as he claps his hands quietly in time to the music. Similarly, Mama Vi smiles broadly and her eyes twinkle with joy as she taps her feet lightly to the music.

Two young men, part of the eleven "ministries" that comprise the morning worship service, form a harmonious duet that surely must please the Lord. "When this tabernacle passes away," they sing (all in Swahili, of course), "we have a new building in heaven, not made with hands."

Then they joyfully conclude their message in song, "We will have a new body." And many hearty *Amens* punctuate their singing.

When three young men follow them in song, Mama Vi explains to her American visitors: "We have been wonderfully surprised and delighted by the way they take Bible stories and put them into song. They are singing now about Samuel and David."

Their song completed, the three young men return to their seats—even as they voice the last words of their story in music.

A mixed trio—two men and a woman—provide the only departure from the norm, in that the men hold a song sheet in front of them as they sing: "Many things make people wonder today, but the greatest wonder of all is that God loves me."

Mama Vi observes: "They have fantastic memories. I constantly marvel at them." The trio continues with their message: "In the body of Christ are many members. The church is the body of Christ. We all work toward one end in Christ. Christ, help me, guide me, I don't want to be an invalid—a babe in Christ.

"We pray and the Lord is working for us," their song continues. "When we welcome visitors, we are welcoming the Lord."

As the singing ceases, an elder of the church comes forward with several announcements. "Pastor," he says, "you can't accomplish anything without work. In the same way, we must work, too.

"All the women of the church will work today, pulling weeds in the garden. We men will work right here in the church. Here we plant 'God's Acre.' The harvest from the rice garden is turned over to the church for the Lord."

As the service nears an end, one of Vinton's assistants walks in with three boxes of literature—Gospels of John in Swahili, from the American Bible Society, printed in Bukavu.

"You can't harvest your crops out there without planting," Pastor Kilongo reminds his listeners. "Let's plant a harvest for Christ, too. We are sick in our bodies, but we are not sick in our hearts."

As the pastor speaks, copies of the Gospels of John are handed out to the eager, excited members of the congregation. A woman with failing eyesight approaches Mama Vi to ask how she can get help so she can read. Marie explains that a Vinton nephew, Fred Gardner, is scheduled to come out to the field in the near future and will be of help with glasses.

After the service, the Kama entourage climbs into the truck, assumes their positions, and the loudspeaker again begins to blare out the Gospel songs the people love to hear.

"We go to minister," Mama Vi observes, "but we're always ministered to. At Christmas time, we always have something special for them—rice, dried fish, oil, soap.

"Each time we go, we hear that one of the older ones has died. When the women get leprosy, often the husbands will put them away. Very few of the children have leprosy."

Opened in 1937, the leper settlement began under control of the Belgian Government, which asked Sam Vinton to direct the work. Kama mission has now been asked to assume full control and supervision. Present director of the leper settlement is Amiu Musa, still under mission supervision.

On the four-mile drive back to Kama, members of a village church waved Baba Vi to a halt. Soon one of the parishioners returned with two eggs—their sacrificial expression of thanks and appreciation to the Vintons for all they mean to the church there.

Arriving at Kama around 11:30 a.m., the travelers climbed out—still moved by the meaningful worship service and the generous spirit of the lepers. On hand to greet Baba Vi at the mission station was an elderly man who had been brought by human carrier for treatment of a badly infected foot. After opening up the wound, Vinton poured in antibiotic salve to draw out the infection.

Counting carriers, some eight or ten nationals then had to take advantage of the extended family principle and stay with a Kama village family while the man recovered.

In the early years of the leper settlement, the population there included upwards of 300 patients and more than 500 other family members, totalling in excess of 800 people.

"You should have seen them," Baba Vi said, "for the most part pagans and dressed like them—fierce looking. They came, but not willingly, preferring to die in their own villages among their own people.

"But the government realized it was time to do some segregating and thus took on this new project.

"We sent out teachers, but they were not welcomed," Vinton added. "The lepers said they had their own heathen religion and they would die with that. They didn't need any teachers from the mission.

"One Christian woman came into the settlement from another mission station and began, in her own humble way, serving and singing in her home. A few women began gathering to hear her sing and give her testimony."

Vinton continued to reminisce. "This went on for some time until one day one of the head men sent word to ask what was the matter with the mission; why weren't they sending out someone to teach them?

"We just said, 'Praise the Lord,' and teachers began to go out to the leper settlement to hold services with them. That was the beginning, and slowly the Word of God took root in hearts and one by one there were believers among them.

"We were fortunate in getting a reclaimed backslider as a 'caretaker and shepherd' of the flock there, and Bernard Mulenda had a real ministry among them. He was not a leper, but lived there with his family in the settlement and was a real spiritual leader."

Mama Vi picked up the story. "Some Christians came from another mission across Lake Tanganyika. They had heard about our Christian leper settlement and wanted to help. They have done a real spiritual work among the people.

"Twenty years earlier, Nurse Mayo was bound for a leper settlement at Lagos, but ill health detained her. Finally, in her advanced years, she came to our leper settlement and was a real mother to these people.

"How she loved them, and they loved her. She certainly laid down her life in their behalf. I know the Lord still has a place for a consecrated nurse among these folks."

Marie then told of visitors from the government to the leper settlement. "Without exception," she said, "they have remarked about the wonderful, joyful spirit among the people—so different from other settlements they have visited.

"The new sulphatrone drugs have been producing marvels. They are very expensive, but the government has been giving them to us and many are encouraged.

"I wish you could see the poor helpless ones—mutilated feet and hands, crawling about. Just to see them come to meetings is something, and then to have others hold the communion cups for them . . . praise the Lord, they are whole in spirit.

"Time and again," Mama Vi continued, "I have heard them testify, 'Praise the Lord that I have His life within.' Or 'praise the Lord, I had to become sick to be made whole again.' "

Marie added, "There is a real burden on our hearts—for the children in the settlement. There have been almost 200 of them. A government doctor said they must send the children back to their villages with relatives, but the parents have refused.

"One boy contracted leprosy, and soon there were nine. All the others were condemned to become lepers unless they were segregated. Through a gift, we built a boys' colony, and had as many as 30 boys at a time. Later, a similar program was begun for the girls."

Meanwhile, the program at the leper settlement continues—and Sam and Marie Vinton keep in close contact with the work there. At every possible opportunity, they visit the settlement and lend their love and encouragement.

While such active programs continue, Baba and Mama Vi seek to accelerate their effectiveness by conducting a literature distribution effort that affects every part of the Kama area ministry.

CHAPTER 11

Preaching by the Printed Page

When 385 Swahili Bibles reached Kama in October 1979 from the Kinshasa Bible House, villagers bought them out in less than two weeks.

That kind of problem, Sam and Marie Vinton admit, is one of the most serious they face, for they hate to turn down people who are eagerly seeking copies of the Word of God. Villagers often walk many miles to obtain copies, only to return empty-handed.

One good example of the desperate need was the experience at the 45th anniversary celebration in Luyamba, previously mentioned, when scores of villagers begged for copies of the Bible—and only 20 copies were available.

It is not that the need is unrecognized by such Bible distribution agencies as the World Home Bible League and Bibles for the World. It is simply, for the most part, a matter of finances and logistics.

"God's Word is quick and powerful," Vinton says, "and the devil knows that. He's fighting its availability and distribution for all he's worth. Many people are willing to pay four days' wages for copies of the Word."

Baba Vi pointed out the fact that their responsibility in the Kama area encompasses some 300,000 people. "For each of our 12 districts," he said, "we should have a large supply of Bibles. We are trying to get the Gideons to open a camp in Kama."

One of the outstanding contributions to Zaire Christian literature came through the herculean efforts of Sam Vinton, Jr., whose book on Bible doctrines has been widely received. Swahili title for the book is *Elimu Kubwa Za Biblia;* French, *Les Grandes Doctrines de la Bible;* English, *Major Doctrines of the Bible.*

Printed in Africa, the volume is clothbound and contains 346 pages. In his review of the book, Chris Egemeier declared it is "characterized by a masterful presentation of the major doctrines of the Bible as viewed from the dispensational concept.

"Diligent research and competent scholarship are clearly evident from cover to cover, but the language used is that of the ordinary

Congo Swahili used by nationals.

"There is no doubt that this work will be of extreme value to African young people who undergo training for Christian service. It will also be most helpful to graduate pastors and missionaries as a source book for the preparation of doctrinal discourses."

Egemeier added: "Based to some extent on Charles F. Baker's 'What We Believe and Why We Believe It,' the new book will fill a long-felt need in Bible institutes and pastors' schools throughout the Swahili-speaking section of the Congo (Zaire) and East Africa. The major doctrines treated in the text are: the Bible, God, Christ, Holy Spirit, angels, man, sin, salvation, the church as the Body of Christ, and prophecy.

"Each chapter ends with a series of review questions. There is a copious and therefore valuable index at the back of the book."

Baba Vi observed: "When some few pastors sought to ban the book it became more sought after than ever.

The book was okayed for general, widespread use when Sam Sr. suggested that instructors using the volume could teach their own views on baptism along with the Grace Mission view.

First printed by the Catholic Press in 1958, the book has now had three printings—the latest by the Africa Inland Mission press.

One of the most valuable supplementary pieces of material employed by the Vintons in their ministry is the Home Study Bible Course on the Gospel of John, which is required for every student in the secondary school. William Ackerman of the World Home Bible League sent 20,000 copies of this course to the Kama mission in 1963, and extremely good use has been made of them.

Other literature donors have included the American Bible Society, Pilgrim Tracts and Scripture Gift Mission. Rochunga Pudaite of Bibles for the World has printed 25,000 copies of the Gospel of John.

Printing of hymnals has been an interesting project, for Sam and Marie Vinton and their co-laborers have had to adapt American hymns to the offbeat rhythms of the Africans, omitting poetic words and phrases in the process.

Youth for Christ meetings in the area first made use of the hymnals, and three of the Vinton children—Sam Jr., Fred and Betty—played an important part in preparation of the books. One idiosyncrasy they had to be on the lookout for: Swahili accent is always on the next-to-last syllable of a word.

Though an occasional familiar tune is recognizable in the churches in Zaire, the trend is away from the American version, for the people love to tell Bible stories in song—Daniel, David and Goliath, Jonah, for example.

More than 10 years ago, a major literature distribution center was begun in Bukavu. Bill Bunch described how this came about:

"Since Mr. Vinton was extremely busy at Kama, Mary (Bill's wife) and I were delegated to help with the literature work in Bukavu. The recovery from the chaotic events of 1967 had been slow.

"However, we were able to reopen our Bible bookstore thanks to a large gift presented by a local Dutch Christian, Mr. Vonk, who fellowshipped with us. Sales stepped up considerably."

Bunch added: "Sales included Bibles in French and Swahili; New Testaments in various languages and other Christian books.

"The distribution of Gospel tracts was held up due to lack of adequate supply. Despite this, however, high school students who stayed at our Protestant Center in Kadutu distributed more than 50,000 tracts."

Bunch added that "the hospital visitation program accounted for another 38,850 leaflets. The pastors at two of our centers (Ibanda and Kadutu) distributed at least 50,000 tracts."

At one time, there were four correspondence courses available in Swahili: John, from the World Home Bible League; Ephesians, by Ernie Green; Romans and Luke, by Chris Egemeier. Many hundreds have completed these courses."

Bunch continued, "We would like to expand this program through the Emmaus courses in French and Lingala as well as the other courses in Swahili.

"Pastor David Sadiki is in charge of the reading room for the main center. Here again is a great opportunity to acquaint national young people with Christian literature. Unfortunately, the supply is extremely limited. There is a real need to have Christian books available in French, Swahili and Lingala."

The needs today are even more acute than they were ten years ago when Bill Bunch gave his report.

"The Ibanda Center is used as a reading room, translation headquarters, correspondence course office, bookstore and apartments for pastors and their families."

Bunch added that "the Nguba Center is used for church services, Sunday school and child evangelism clubs.

With regard to translation work, Bunch added: "This was a new department. Sam Vinton, Jr. was responsible for the training of two nationals, Pastors Enock Paul and Ipuma Christien.

"These young men have had special training in Bible study, analysis and language work."

About a year after these urgent literature needs were shared, Sam Vinton Sr. gave a report of slight improvement in the availability of much-needed printed matter:

"The Scripture text calendars from Christian Service in New Jersey are a real blessing and a tremendous witness. We have received about 8,000 of them free. I airmailed these folks a Swahili Bible so they could copy out the appropriate verses.

"Pilgrim Tract Society has another three tons of Gospel tracts ready to ship. I wrote them to be sure to print the tracts in large type and open pages (wide margins). Their Kilalo tract is perhaps the best I've seen for the Africans. We're using it for memory work, especially among the girls and women whom Marie teaches."

Vinton added: "We're working on the new edition of the Gospel of John. The Bible Society will pay expenses and sell them to us about 50 percent off the selling price. We're hoping to get a printing of 25,000.

"We have received the silk book markers and appreciate them so much. We can use many more of these, with the Scripture verses relating to special headings: ministry, dedication, faithfulness, witnessing, etc."

Vinton reported, "We have received a copy of the new Swahili songbook and Maneno 16 (16 *Things About Faith*). These booklets with their large, clear type and open pages are tops.

"I am working with Pastor Etienne Katamea to use these booklets in the Bible hour of the fifth and sixth years in all of our primary schools.

We're completely out of the Ephesians and Romans course, but have a small supply of John on hand.

"These courses, put into our fifth and sixth years as official texts in our religious classes, can be greatly used of God in the lives of these students. We have more than 700 in those two classes alone."

Just a few years earlier, immediately following the rebellion, Vinton reported a drastic literature picture that slowly began to see some improvement:

"We have nothing in our bookshops—no new arrivals since before the rebels came in the middle of 1964. In fact, we have just decided to close down the bookshop at the Theological Center and transform the place into a reading room.

"What books we might use from Dar es Salaam or Nairobi cost about ten times what our people can pay because of the low value of the Congo franc on the world market. This also holds true for books from Belgium, Switzerland and France.

"To spend a whole day's salary for a little booklet, which at the official rate of exchange would cost only the tenth of a day's salary, certainly makes it hard, if not impossible, for these fellows to buy anything but local or highly subsidized books."

Vinton then gave an example of the effect of inflation on books: "Plastic-covered Bibles, which we formerly sold for 300 francs, now cost 1,000 francs. There has been a 300 to 500 percent increase in prices in the Congo, while salaries have increased only 50 to 100 percent.

"Mission presses in the Congo (one in the northern part of the Kivu Province; the other in the Katanga Province) are slowly getting back into production and will produce some much-needed literature."

Vinton added, "However, there is no surface transportation to speak of, and the cost of shipping books and tracts by air is prohibitive. The only apparent solution to the problem is for the missionaries and staff of Grace Mission to prepare their own books in the Swahili language and have them printed at the lowest possible cost.

"Sam Vinton Jr., Chris Egemeier and Ernie Green have been working on this project for the past 10 years. Some books have already been prepared, while others are still in the making. One does not write a book in a day, or even in a month's time—it is a slow process."

Baba Vi added this appeal: "Friends in America can pray for God's help and blessing on these book-writing projects."

Still today good Christian books and magazines are avidly devoured and enjoyed. And, because the literature need is so desperate, Vinton's timely appeal to supporters and friends is worth repeating:

"How many of us at one time or another have felt the desire to be a missionary? Yet how few really reach the foreign field. Today it is possible for everyone of us to be a literature missionary and through the printed word reach the multitudes for Christ.

"Why not let God use you to send the printed word into thousands and thousands of homes, into village after village, in our great Zaire field?

"Even if it were possible for you to come to Zaire today, it would still be impossible for you to take a witness into these homes and villages in darkness behind the rebel lines. Yet through the printed word carried by the nationals, you can reach them for Christ by being a literature missionary.

"We definitely believe that Christian literature is God's means for reaching men and women for Christ in this space age.

"Jehovah's Witnesses are enrolled in literature distribution. Communism sends out millions of pieces of literature. We who have. the Word of God should now mass our resources and manpower and. launch a great literature distribution crusade."

Baba Vi concluded, "To do this we need literature missionaries with the vision of reaching every home in every village with the Gospel in our great Zaire field.

"Be a missionary!"

Some things have been done, and are being done, to try to meet the urgent needs. When Chris Egemeier wrote a tract, "Are You

Saved?" in the Swahili language, Grace Mission printed 90,000 copies for shipment to Zaire. Though that helped immensely, a great need still remains.

Egemeier also compiled an 84-page Scripture Memory Course and prepared a commentary on the Pastoral Epistles, both in Swahili. This and other literature made possible a number of home Bible classes in and around Bukavu, under the direction of Ernest Green. They not only proved fruitful, but also led to successful children's meetings.

At this writing, Egemeier is living in Florida but *still writing Swahili Literature.* His two big books, *Waroma* (commentary on the book of Romans) and *Habari Ya Kanisa* (a history of the church) should be off the Mission Presses in 1981.

Prior to his great success in writing a Bible doctrine book in Swahili, Sam Vinton Jr. met with language experts concerned about translating the Bible and other Gospel literature for the benefit of nationals in their various areas.

"The Bible Translators' Seminar, held in Kinshasa was tremendous," Sam Jr. reported.

"Real topnotch men, such as Dr. Eugene Nida, Dr. Taber, Dr. Reyburn and others, directed the sessions. We also had a Swiss pastor, the Rev. Margot, who is presently translating the New Testament into vernacular French."

Sam Jr. continued, "Actually, it is the French equivalent to the Today's English Version put out by the Bible Society. Pastor Margot has been very skillful in getting us into actual translation problems and involving us in seeking solutions.

"Or course, Drs. Nida and Taber were terrific. We have discussed many things that are really helpful. I appreciated this course very much and it will help me a great deal in my own writing, let alone Bible translation.

"There were 75 delegates from all over Zaire, plus one from Togo and four from Madagascar. Accompanying me to the seminar were Pastors Paul Wakanga, Albert Mukula and Urbano Tambwe. They profited much from the sessions."

Sam Jr. added that staff members came from the United States, England and other countries. In addition, Bible Society consultants came from all parts of Africa.

"We had a special meeting with Dr. Nida and Dr. Fehderau (the Bible Society consultant from Zaire) to commence organizing our Swahili committee. Plans will be formulated for the work on a new Bible translation.

"The Bible Society is not interested in a simple revision of the existing Swahili Bible, but would like a completely new translation. The officials would discourage us from following the original (or

English and French) text word for word, thus making it too literal and loaded down with our way of expressing things. This is why they are interested in a completely new and Africanized translation."

The younger Vinton then detailed the seminar procedure. "Our daily schedule opened at 8:15 a.m. with 15 minutes of devotions, followed by four classes in the morning.

"We had one class in the afternoon, then almost two hours of practical work such as translating passages from Mark, Luke, John and Romans, or discussing linguistic problems. Each language group met separately; I was the leader of the Swahili group.

Sam Vinton Sr. feels that the vital importance of Christian literature in the missionary program cannot be overemphasized. Facts and figures seem to substantiate his contention.

In one three-month period at the Bukavu reading room, for example, 8,017 people visited the facilities and 37 made decisions for Christ. Directors of the reading room explained:

"Each reading room is stocked with both paper and hard-bound books, booklets and magazines in various languages. Each room also has a rack for free literature and is kept supplied with Gospel tracts in French, Swahili, Moshi, Lingala and Kilega. There are tables and chairs where the visitors may read, study or write.

"Most of those persons using the facilities of the reading rooms are students. They drop in to study from their own textbooks, or to browse over the available reading material."

The report continued, "Even though they cannot read English, they enjoy the pictures in such magazines as *National Geographic, Holiday* and similar travel magazines. Quite a few Europeans drop in to look around and ask questions of the pastor in charge.

"Roman Catholic priests and nuns have visited the reading rooms, some even buying Bibles and New Testaments in the adjoining bookstore.

"A national pastor is in charge of each reading room. He endeavors to engage readers in quiet conversation regarding the importance of receiving the Lord Jesus Christ as Saviour."

Concluding, the directors observed, "He also has to keep a sharp watch on the movements of the readers, as books and magazines often disappear with amazing rapidity. Some of those caught sneaking out with a stolen book or magazine under the arm or stashed in a briefcase (the status symbol of a student!) have been convicted of their guilt and their consequent need of a Saviour.

"The reading room ministry has thus proved to be another effective channel for reaching lost souls for Christ."

Small wonder that Sam Vinton is seriously concerned about the present lack of good Gospel literature in Zaire.

On returning from his twelfth trip to the Zaire field, Henry

Sonneveldt came away with a new burden for the literature need—especially Swahili Bibles, so greatly in demand. When he presented the need to his own Grand Rapids congregation, several thousand dollars came in for sending Swahili Bibles to Sam and Marie Vinton for distribution.

The Vintons greatly dislike having to turn down strong pleas for the Word of God, especially knowing that many thousands of Americans have Bibles in abundance, a sizeable number of them merely gathering dust.

Formal education is another important facet of the overall ministry of the Vintons. Zaire's church of tomorrow is being trained in this way.

CHAPTER 12

Education in Kama

"The schools have literally been turned upside down in Zaire following the nationalization of 1971," reported 17-year-old Steve Vinton, son of George and Dawn Vinton, in 1978, after his first visit to the field. Proud grandparents Sam and Marie justifiably glow at the young man's accomplishments.

"Before nationalization, the Bible institute here at Kama, where I am now teaching, not only had such basic necessities as chalk, paper and textbooks, but also a beautifully equipped library.

"Now when the government returned the schools to the Mission, we find not only no library, but no textbooks, and yes, even a roofless building. I personally have the only two math books that exist here at Kama.

"Why would God allow the government to nationalize our mission schools, and then after failing to provide any education for four years, return them in such an impossible state? It's pretty depressing, right? Wrong!

"I used to feel that way as I would stand and watch the sun set on the roofless building, but now I know better. A student of mine put it all into perspective for me. 'You would have to be blind not to see that when you throw the missionaries out, when you throw religion out, when you throw God out, things just don't work.' "

Steve added: "It took the Zaire government four years to realize that, but if the government can realize that, if the Zairois themselves can realize that, then can we not also be expected to realize that? The mission is needed as never before; the government proved that.

"I've been working here for almost a year now, teaching advanced Calculus and Analytical Geometry to the seniors, and Algebra and Euclidean Geometry to the freshmen. It's been a real challenge for me, being a 17-year-old, just out of high school. But God gave me the work, and He is in it.

"I don't, of course, just teach math. I am reminded of what Jesus said in His sermon on the mount, 'Let your light so shine before men . . .' (Matthew 5:16). Can an educated man of the twentieth

93

century *not* believe in evolution, and better yet, can he back up his beliefs with scientific evidence?"

The Vintons' grandson continued, "Is it possible for him *not* to be be an existentialist? Can he really be sure of the existence of God, and finally can he believe Jesus Christ to be the Son of God? My students are finding out; yes, they are starting to think, and to challenge things they previously held to be true, The seed has thus been planted.

"It should be known that the majority of our 7,000 students do not attend church and have little intention of doing so. The school is our avenue to reach them."

Young Vinton added: "The government, in an about-face, is now trying to force Christianity back into the schools by demanding religion classes twice a week. Clearly, God has opened the door.

"Can we say no—that we lack the resources or the time? What excuse will be sufficient when the harvest is lacking?

"Help us as we work to meet this need. We need five French-speaking Christian teachers for the years ahead. This year I am here alone. Next year I can't say that I will be here. Can you pray that the need will be met?

"Pray also for the students and those in positions of authority, for the educational, financial and spiritual needs of the school, that our schools might once again bring honor to His Name."

Such thinking on the part of a young man who has seen the need firsthand is one of the most encouraging factors Sam and Marie Vinton have experienced in a long time.

Two years earlier, when Steve visited the mission station for the first time, he was overwhelmed with the experience—so much so that he wrote some very stirring and graphic words ·in the Vinton guestbook just before his departure. He had no idea, of course, that his emotional entry would be captured by a visiting writer and shared with thousands of others.

"Kama is indeed a wonderful place! Though this beautiful place is but a dot on the map in an area much of the world knows little about, Kama shall always occupy a special place in my heart.

"It's not so much *where* Kama is, although Africa is far away from America and beyond the reach of most. Rather it is what Kama symbolizes that makes it so special.

"Kama represents the past that my father so enjoyed—a past that still lives; in the places where he played, learned and experienced so much; but most of all, in the people that he knew and grew up with."

Steve's clearly legible writing continued, "Kama represents progress and hope for the future. Necessity and lack are solved through ingenuity and determination—that has certainly been proved by Kama's success. Many things were started and perfected at Kama before the rest of this country even thought—or saw the need—of them.

"Kama represents the life of my grandparents much more than any other place in the world. It is in this area that these special people have spent much of their lives together. They have gone through, and endured, the rebellions, the mercenaries, the bad times, when others would have given up."

Steve added: "Instead they weathered the storm and showed through their actions that God's people don't have to be quitters. These people have anguished and suffered along with the people here as terror spread many times across the country. Through their faith they provided a beacon of light to comfort those in need.

"Kama represents this . . . and much more. But most important of all, Kama represents an *idea,* a *vision,* a *goal!* Many decades ago, it was a young man joined by the woman he loved who set out to shape and mold a self-sufficient Christian community based on God's principles.

"With the Bible in one hand and the capacity for work in the other, they brought the light of God to a dark world and the opportunity for progress in an undeveloped land. The remarkable thing is that it worked and their goals are being met."

Steve then pointed to the reason behind his grandparents' success. "God has worked mightily in this land and the message of God's love has been firmly planted. It is because Kama rests on such a foundation—a strong foundation—that it continues to thrive and move forward.

"This is the message that Kama sends out to the rest of the world. Not only must individuals have a strong foundation found only in Christ, but so also must the society!"

Young Vinton continued, "Kama has not, of course, been without problems—and sometimes its successes have caused other problems—but Kama *has* made progress. Working to meet the pressing needs of the body, and of the mind, and of the spirit, these two missionaries have helped the people in ways and degrees immeasurable.

"So now, on the eve of my departure, as I look back over the past few weeks, I realize how much I will miss Kama. It has become home. The safaris have become something to look forward to—an opportunity to help in the limited way I could; a chance to get to know my Grandpa, learn of his past and of his plans for the future; a chance to experience.

"Coming to Kama meant a lot—leaving means spending time with my Grandma (a brief trip to Europe together)—someone I can now count not as just my Grandma but also my friend. Yes, Kama means a lot to me—both the pineapples and the bridges, the good and not so good."

Steve concluded: "I shall miss the people whom I've come to know and love. I shall miss the mud huts and the holes in the roads. I shall miss and long for these days past that have been some of the greatest I've yet experienced.

"I cannot thank the people of Kama enough for accepting me as a friend and I shall miss my new-found popularity! I've seen God work miraculously to get me here, to provide me with a friend in England, and to keep me safe.

"Kama and my visit to it have taught me things I will never forget. I thank you for opening your home and your hearts to me. May God continue to bless you bountifully. With love, Steve."

For every young person—with that kind of love and commitment—called to the educational program at Kama, Sam and Marie Vinton are convinced their efforts will be multiplied a hundredfold. So much can be accomplished with so few—provided there is real dedication and perseverance.

In a 75-mile radius around Kama, some 10,000 students are the mission's responsibility. "Three-fourths of the students are not getting the gospel, yet they are open and eager for the Word," the Vintons say.

"The church must take action. We must get the New Testament into the hands of every student, and we must set up Home Study Bible Courses."

As recently as ten years ago, the school situation had some very encouraging signs. Bill Bunch described the unusual activity, predictably in the area where Sam and Marie Vinton labor so effectively:

"The elementary teachers and students, plus high school teachers and students, planned and conducted the entire Sunday morning services at Kama for a full month.

"Everyone was happy to see how well the program was prepared and presented. The result? Youth teams go out into the village churches each weekend. The response was so good that there are now 13 youth teams with about 6 students each."

Bunch continued: "The first phase was to meet with our co-laborers for Christ. Pastor Albert Mukula, director of the Kama Bible School, and Pastor Yakobo Bitingo, director of the Kama Evangelistic Department.

"We coordinated our youth teams with the Bible school's evangelistic campaigns and the weekend evangelistic services. After prayer and discussion, a schedule was set up which follows a map of the local area around our Kama station here in the jungle of Zaire.

"Names like Pene-Kusu, Mamboleo, Bukama and Idumu do not

mean much to you, but to us they mean villages where people need to be encouraged in the Lord and hear the Gospel of God's grace."

In that ideal, coordinated effort, church and school worked together not only to educate but also to evangelize. Sam and Marie Vinton hope for a return of that kind of close-knit cooperation that is made possible only by having sufficient personnel to do the job.

"The second phase," Bunch continued, "was to interest others in the supervision of these teams. After much prayer, several people were contacted.

"The Lord was working in hearts, for the entire high school faculty expressed a desire to help guide, train and supervise these young men and women (praise the Lord, we have five girls who have joined a team)."

Bunch added, "The two primary school directors and the school secretaries also volunteered. Their role is to assist and sponsor the youth teams. Each Saturday the team for that Sunday presents its program to its sponsor.

"The sponsor will go with his team and can take an active part in the Sunday service if he wishes to do so. After returning, he must give an oral report to us of the activities of the team. We now have 11 sponsors to help organize and carry on this program of guiding these young people."

Bunch pointed out that the third phase was a weekly training program. "This was not only for their Christian education, but also to encourage them and keep up their interest. Our first session was for information and to give a model program, set up by the four-year team (10th year high school).

"Guess what happened. Several old people from Kama heard the singing, thought it was a special meeting and came in to listen. Afterwards, there was an open discussion for questions and comments. It was thrilling to see the group showing their classmates how to conduct a service.

"Their program was then revised, corrected and typed. Each team received a notebook in which the model program was attached. All the teams are called *Amis de Christ* (Friends of Christ)."

Adding that each team selected its own biblical name, Bunch continued: "In their notebook, each captain listed all team members. During each trip he is to write a report of his team's experiences and activities.

"He is also to jot down the names of each tract or Christian booklet for distribution. Literature packets include: 'Help from Above'; 'Fourteen Things About Christ'; 'Friend' (all in Swahili); and "Choose Life' (in French)."

The fourth phase, Bunch added, is getting the youth teams out into the forest villages. "The first team, the 'Faithfuls,' broke the ice by going out to the leper settlement.

"We borrowed an old truck, and I went along with their director, Alimasi Gaston. We sang as we bounced along the jungle road. The local pastor had been notified of our coming and just about everyone was at the meeting on time.

"Others, without toes and fingers, took longer to hobble in. We were welcomed by happy, smiling faces, some of which were distorted by the ravages of this terrible disease. They had a song in their hearts and praise on their lips for Christ and His love for them."

Bunch continued, "They sang for us and then took the offering: firewood, rice, manioc and some little money the people had. Then the 'Faithfuls' took over. What a joy to hear beautiful three-part harmony from these young men.

"I spoke on Jonah and Christ. I told them how Jonah went *down* to flee from the face of God and how Christ went *up* to pray face to face with God. Abedy Willermond gave his testimony, which was really a sermon of 25 minutes!

"He told them about prayer, its importance, when to pray, what to pray for and how to pray. After the service, the students and sponsor distributed the booklets and tracts. We sang all the way home."

Other have played a vital part in the on-going educational program at Kama. One of these, Lennart Anderson, who worked closely with the Vintons for several years, gave a report prior to his return to the States in 1971:

"As my year of building has come to an end and I am ready to return to my family, I am glad to report that all of the secondary school building has been constructed.

"The metal roof covers all of the new walls. The last section was roofed just in time to keep the rains from damaging the walls, laid in mud mortar."

Anderson added: "Two of the classrooms and the library are in service. Four other classrooms have been leveled and the bricks laid—ready for the cement work. The office and the teachers' lounge are also ready.

"The fill in the two other classrooms and the long hallway are in the process of being completed by the secondary school students. The final building will result in a series of three units, containing ten classrooms, an office, teachers' lounge, library and laboratory, with washrooms on either end of the long unit.

"The entire population has expressed appreciation for the building and for the quality of construction that has gone into the building. As a self-aid project, there has been much participation by the church and the community."

Tremendous amounts of fill for the floors have been brought in by women of the community, Anderson added. "Students from the primary school have also helped in this. Others have been instrumental in tearing down the old walls of the Imonga mining camp to obtain bricks for the construction—some 400,000 bricks.

"Men have given their time to rebuild the road going to the camp so that the trucks bringing the bricks could pass. Other villages have donated several loads of sand for the cement work. The secondary school students helped with the digging of the foundations.

"They will continue until all the ground around the school is properly leveled and landscaped. All this brings us to the conclusion that this is no small project, and we are glad to see it nearing completion."

Anderson added that all in all the construction is a source of pride to the entire community, and the people appreciate the help that the United States Government has given to make such a school building possible.

"It is the only secondary school for more than 70 miles in any direction. It serves a tremendous need.

"The original plan called for a school of some six classrooms, but we found that it was wise to expand it, so that now we have ten classrooms, a library, a laboratory, a teachers' lounge and an office.

"This gives a total of 1200 square meters of floor space. We also have ready for future completion washrooms for boys and girls at either end of the building. I believe that AID (Agency for International Development) has gotten their money's worth, both in material and in good will."

That kind of practical help is invaluable, and more is needed on a regular basis. Sam and Marie Vinton's workload would be significantly eased with the addition of part-time or full-time missionaries to assist in every phase of the work—certainly several could be used in the educational field.

Scattered across the length and breadth of the country of Zaire are hundreds, yea thousands, of men and women who passed through the schools of Kama and came out as believers in the Lord Jesus Christ. While that work continues today, it remains a frustration to Baba and Mama Vi, for they realize only the surface is being scratched in comparison with the potential.

Educationally, Zaire had only 16 university graduates at the time of independence, not counting those who had done their university studies in theology. The country had adopted a philosophy of beginning at the grassroots level to provide an elementary education for everyone, slowly working up to the university level.

Primary school attendance has jumped from 65 percent of Zaire's children in 1960 to 85 percent today. Secondary school enrollment rose from 1 percent to 8 percent. Mission organizations have run

Zaire's schools since the earliest colonial period.

"Even though the Zairian children are not required by law to attend school, most parents have come to value education so much that they will sacrifice, cheat, bribe—do almost anything—to get their children in school," Sam Vinton Jr. pointed out.

"Unfortunately, sometimes they must do all three if they are to find a place for their children in school."

In January 1974, the government educational department took over control of the schools and complete chaos resulted. Finally, in 1977, the government asked the churches to assume operation of the schools again, as young Steve Vinton noted.

Rundown buildings, low morale and lack of discipline complicated the churches' task, and an earnest effort is being made today to restore some semblance of order in the schools.

"Our schools were built on the Bible," Baba Vi says. "Memory work was emphasized, and New Testaments were given away as contest awards."

At one time, back in the sixties, a women's school was an active force in the area. Becky Vinton, wife of Sam Jr., described that phase of the work:

"I was very happy to be able to go down to Kama to set up the women's school once again. Yoane Ignace and his wife are in charge. We have two schools, incidentally—one for beginning readers and one for advanced readers, with a total attendance of 137 women.

"Yoane teaches reading, writing, hygiene, good manners, Bible and homemaking. Two young women are now teaching the sewing classes.

"Yoane has been sending me encouraging reports concerning the progress of the two schools. I was wondering how they would manage without close supervision, so I am very pleased that there have been no big problems thus far."

Becky added: "I know that they are trusting the Lord to guide them and give them the wisdom they need.

"I prepare the lessons for Yoane to teach and send the sewing projects down, after first meeting with the teachers and showing them what to do. I have been able to get some very good and helpful books from Kenya, written in East African Swahili.

"We go through these books and change any really different words into the better known Congo (Zaire) Swahili."

Continuing her report, Becky said: "Our women teachers work with the sewing projects. They seem to be doing a very good job.

"Requests are coming in from other sections of the Kama territory for additional schools of this nature. However, we just don't have the funds or personnel necessary to establish them.

"Sam (Jr.) took down several packages of visual aid materials that

I had prepared for Kama, Mwanga and Kasongo. I hope to begin a type of lending library of visual aids at Kama. Right now, I'm working on 'The Lives of the Patriarchs' and 'The Life of Christ.'"

Becky added that "these lessons were sent out to me in the drums (steel barrels) and I am putting each scene on a flash card poster. This way the figures won't get lost and we don't have to make flannelgraph boards.

"Hallie Green followed this procedure for Ernie's Bible classes and it worked very nicely. She had some very good ideas. I hope to go through the whole Bible in this manner for the pastors and teachers to use in the Kama area.

"We have adapted Bible lessons which were translated into Swahili by the Child Evangelism Fellowship in Bujumbura, Burundi."

In many instances, yesteryear looks much brighter than the present picture in the field of education, insofar as Zaire is concerned. Sam and Marie Vinton are hoping that scores of young people will respond to the present need—out of a heart commitment to the spiritual needs of people in a different part of the world.

Some of the Vintons' co-laborers have been identified already. Others—equally important—have made invaluable contributions to the work, including their own children and other relatives.

101

CHAPTER 13

They Help Hold the Fort

"The old proverb, 'Before you criticize you should walk for one mile in the other person's shoes,' is a solid piece of advice for anyone, especially in dealing with people in other cultures and countries."

So stated Dr. Richard B. Nymeyer, of Lynden, Washington, after he and his family had made their first trip to Zaire. The highly capable chiropractor and able missionary is considered by Sam and Marie Vinton a valued co-laborer in the work at the Kama station.

Similarly, they highly value the daily performance of his wife Jane, who does far more than merely raise three fine children: Jaylene, Julie and Jennifer.

"When we arrived in Zaire," Rich said, "and especially after we settled down in Kama, the need for the application of this principle became very apparent. We saw many things that were hard to understand according to our 'western way' of thinking.

"For example, why doesn't the national milk that goat or use those chicken eggs for breakfast? We also saw things being done that seemed toilsome and overburdening. Why do the women walk so far into the forest to their fields and each day return those same long distances with heavy burdens on their backs and heads?"

Nymeyer added, "We saw people paying $1.25 a quart for kerosene so they could study after the work day. They made approximately $15 a month so you can see they must really want to study to do that.

"It would be like someone in the United States who makes $1500 a month spending $125 to buy a quart of kerosene.

"Other people asked us for candles to burn at night when the owl hooted to protect them from the witches. (The owl was believed to be the scout for the witch by which she was led to her victim. The candlelight scared the owl away, so they believed.)"

Continuing his story, Rich declared: "It was not until we had literally walked where they walked and carried what they carried and worked beside them that we began to understand the reasons behind these actions and God burdened our hearts to do something about it.

"For example, concerning their fear of witches and evil spirits. Where can they find strength except in a secure relationship with God, fortified by His Spirit through His Word, which says, 'Greater is He that is in you than he that is in the world.'?

"How will they be strengthened except by being fed with the milk of the Word and then as they grow, learn to study and dig out the meat of the Word for themselves?"

Nymeyer added: "They need someone for this, not only to share the plan of salvation, but also they need a Bible to study and Bible study lessons to help them grow. They also need the time, ability and tools to do the studying at night after their work in the fields is done.

"Remember, they do not have daylight saving time, so that after 6:30 p.m. it is dark and a light is necessary if one wants to study. A diet sufficient in protein is also necessary for mental development if the studying is to be worthwhile.

"Our desire is that every person shall have the opportunity to receive Christ and then grow in the knowledge of God and in the position and responsibilities we have in Christ.

"Major hindrances include an insufficient supply of Bibles and Bible study guides and aids for all who desire them; lack of time and ability to study, comprehend and apply what is studied and understand how it could change their lives."

Sam Vinton is indeed a "living legend," and many marvel that God has indeed done so much through one man. They consider Marie an integral part of all that has been done and is being done at Kama.

When Becky and Sam Jr. left the field in 1976, it was to fill an urgent Bible teaching need at Grace Bible College in Grand Rapids. Their original intention was to serve there for only two years, but they find their tour of duty there so needful and rewarding that they remain in that key spot.

The eight-week GYM (Grace Youth Ministries) fresh water project had a tremendous effect on village life in and around the Kama area. Work teams, paired with the nationals in the usual Vinton participation policy, labored together until noon—helping the village people to drill their own wells by use of the Hydro-Drill.

Afternoons were devoted to football (soccer), with competition between mixed black-white teams rather than Americans against the Africans. In the evenings, open-air meetings featured songs, testimonies and Gospel films.

Candidates for the GYM (Grace Youth Ministries) program had to undergo a strong orientation program and study Swahili as a special requirement. They also had studies in spiritual development, interpersonal relationships, theology of missions, cross-cultural differences and communication. They had to read a lot of books about the country; be active in their own churches prior to coming, and had to have references from their pastors and at least three others outside their immediate families.

Always a possibility with such a program was that one or more of the young people might see the desperate need and sense a call to the field. Surely the need is great, for many of the older missionaries have retired and have not yet been replaced.

Take Chris and Edna Mae Egemeier, for example. Sam and Marie Vinton speak glowingly of their working days together. When the Egemeiers returned to the field in 1970 to work in Bukavu with the Sam Vintons Jr., they cited the need, the opportunities and the time as their reasons for returning.

"Right now," the Egemeiers said, "we feel this is the time for us to return, since certain obstacles have been removed, and the way things have been moving both here at home and on the field, with so many dear friends rallying to our support, it seems we are right about this."

Pastor Bilembo Amuri's dramatic testimony indicates something of the impact the Egemeiers have had in thousands of African lives.

"I was believed dead," he declared, "but I came back to life.

"In 1938, I was born in the village of Mukulukusu, a member of the Warega tribe. I completed my primary school education in 1960, when Mr. Egemeier was the school director.

"However, while I was still a child, I received Jesus Christ as my Saviour. Because of this early decision, I had a hunger for learning the Word of God, although I still followed the way of the world."

Pastor Amuri continued: "My marriage to a Christian girl took place in 1963, and we were blessed with a son the following year.

"That year, 1964, the terrible trouble started. It was the time of the Mulele rebellion throughout Zaire. When the rebels neared our village, we fled for our lives.

"But the Muleles were too fast for us. Amidst the fierce fighting, 17 of our people were killed. My child and I were captured in a trap set by the rebels. Three other persons, a man and two women, were also taken prisoners."

Continuing his story, Pastor Amuri said: "Filled with fright and worry, we were dragged and pulled from the forest to the road. There the enemy callously killed one of the two women. That left four of us, including my baby. What was going to happen to us?

"When we arrived at the road barrier near Kapulu-unga, all of us were badly beaten by our captors. They took my dear child out of my arms, then forced the three of us to march to Kampene, headquarters of a mining company.

"Here they separated the man and the woman from me. They were to stay there. I was taken all the way to Kasongo, more than

200 kilometers (about 130 miles) from my home. Any hope I had of being rescued died right then. I was thrown into the local prison at Kasongo, where I cried to God to save me."

Pastor Amuri added: "There were many other prisoners with me. Some of them said to me, 'Why are you praying to God, when we are just waiting here to be killed?' They warned me that the Muleles did not believe in God and did not want His name to be mentioned.

"But this only made me pray more earnestly. I prayed not just for myself, but also for my family and friends, and for my dear baby.

"One fellow prisoner, Ndalabu, told me to get out of there with my God. 'Don't you know we are in danger of dying?' he asked. My response was to start praying for him. 'Oh, God,' I prayed, 'help me and Ndalabu, too, so that he might believe that you are the one true God."

Pastor Amuri continued: "God helped Ndalabu right then to believe. 'Truly your God is the true God,' he said. Soon many prisoners were praying with me.

"After three weeks, God delivered us. First a colonel of the army came and took me out of the prison and put me in his own house. Then a detachment of government troops arrived in Kasongo and defeated the rebels and all of the prisoners were set free. Transportation was arranged to return the captives to their home villages.

"You can imagine the astonishment and joy that greeted my return to my village. Shouts of 'He's come back from the dead!' were all about me as I greeted and embraced relatives and friends."

The pastor concluded: "None of them thought that I could have survived the beatings and imprisonment. Joy of joys, my wife and child were still alive and we were united as a family. How faithful our God is!

"Since then, I have tried to be faithful, too, as a good servant of the Lord Jesus Christ. I am pastor of a local congregation and I love to preach God's Word. It's a wonderful feeling to 'come back from the dead.' "

Multiply Pastor Amuri's story scores of times, and some idea of the effective ministry of missionaries like the Vintons and the Egemeiers can be imagined.

William D. Bunch, now director of program development for Grace Mission, with headquarters in Grand Rapids, with his wife Mary served in Zaire for 16 years—in various capacities (teaching, administration, inspection, and training seminars). They have played a vital role in the ongoing ministry of Sam and Marie Vinton.

Many other missionaries could be cited for their work in Zaire with the Vintons, but an intentional effort is being made to stick to the story of Baba and Mama Vi primarily.

Perhaps the darkest period of the Vintons' missionary career, the days of rebellion, proved the perseverance of Sam and Marie and the faithfulness of their God.

CHAPTER 14

Days of Rebellion

Chaotic days in the history of Kama mission began when some of the Congolese attended the World's Fair in Belgium in 1958 and first became conscious of several moves for independence in neighboring countries.

That began considerable political activity in the Congo, and violent riots erupted in Leopoldville (now Kinshasa) in January 1959. Eventually, that led to a coalition government just days before "Independence Day"—June 30, 1960—with Patrice Lumumba as Prime Minister and Joseph Kasavubu in the relatively powerless position of President.

These hectic days began a time of increasing turmoil for Sam and Marie Vinton and their colleagues, who persevered and prayed for peace in the land.

Lawlessness, anarchy, rebellion, revolt and secession followed in rapid order:

July 8, 1960: Moise Tshombe, provincial president of Katanga, employed Belgian troops when the army rebelled.

July 10, 1960: Lumumba condemned the Belgian invasion.

July 11, 1960: Lumumba asked for the aid of UN troops.

July 13, 1960: The Security Council ordered Belgian withdrawal.

July 15-18, 1960: UN troops numbering 3,500 arrived.

September 1960: President Kasavubu "fired" Lumumba, who countered by relieving Kasavubu of his office. Joseph Mobutu, 28, seized the government, ousted Kasavubu and Lumumba, and closed Parliament.

December 1960: Stanleyville became legal capital of the Congo. Mobutu now controlled Leopoldville and two provinces: Lumumba, the rest of the Congo except Tshombe's secessionist Katanga Province.

January 1961: Mobutu, with the approval of Kasavubu, transferred Lumumba to Katanga to prevent his escape. Meanwhile, Kasavubu, re-established as President by Mobutu, named Joseph Ileo as Prime Minister.

February 1961: When Lumumba was killed while trying to escape, UN diplomats ordered Congolese to straighten out their own affairs or face strict UN control, politically and militarily.

April 1961: Tshombe promised to discharge his mercenaries, easing the fighting, but then he bolstered his forces.

September 1961: UN forces brought Tshombe under control, but tens of thousands of Baluba people were killed or starved to death during the conflict. Tshombe exiled to Europe.

June 1961-June 1964: When the Congo split into 24 small provinces, the power of the chieftains increased. During three army revolts, soldiers turned on Kasavubu and Mobutu, physically beating them. When Kasavubu was able to seize the initiative, he named Tshombe to lead a new government.

September 1964-October 1965: Tshombe mustered mercenary soldiers from a number of world nations to reduce Lumumbist rebel control. Communist-supported forces retaliated by taking white hostages, who suffered torture and death.

November 1965: Mobutu seized power again on November 25, discharging Kasavubu and declaring himself as President for a five-year term. He changed the name of the country to Zaire.

Miraculously, amidst all the confusion and bloodshed, Sam and Marie Vinton escaped serious injury and found ways to serve their friends in Zaire.

When circumstances forced them from troubled areas, they moved across the border until calm was restored—all the while seeking ways to rehabilitate the villages for which they felt responsible. They had learned to love the land and the people; they must help in any way they could.

The nationals did not escape unharmed, nor did their villages.

"The situation at Kama is very sad," wrote pastor-evangelist Yokobo Bitingo in the mid-sixties. "This station is completely empty and deserted. Our enemies burned every village from Kampene to Kama (about 55 miles); then on the road from Kama to Kampungu (about 45 miles) they also burned every village.

"From Lusumba to Tanganyika (about 40 miles), every village was destroyed and burned.

"All of our teachers are safe, except Pastors John Kifunza, Augustin Mikonge and Bernard Mulenda, who were captured by the rebels. We have not heard whether these men are alive or dead."

Pastor Albert Mukula, director of the Kama Bible Institute, added: "The first group of rebels who came to Kama stayed only one day. But another group came from Wazimba territory and they burned all the villages and all the houses at Kama Mission, except the houses of the missionaries.

"And they are still there, as far as I know, unless the soldiers have come and driven them off. As for the people, there was much fighting and many were killed, especially in the Beia section.

"There, Chief Andrea Kibonge and Chief Kitingi (the Christian chief) were killed, also one of the teachers who used to be at Kaseke. Emille Kingombe, yes, and my own younger brother, Daniel."

God worked mightily through the days of rebellion, and in 1962 Sam and Marie Vinton experienced one of many miracles.

"We were in Bukavu to pick up the Egemeiers," Baba Vi said. "Just as we were ready to take off for Kama, we received word the bridge was out. So we began to redeem the time by looking for New Testaments."

Unsuccessful in their search, that spurred a clear leading from the Lord for the Vintons to go back to Bukavu at the first opportunity and establish a literature center. Too, Sam felt the need for a guest house for missionaries to come and rest. They began to pray.

Encountering Madame Bia DeKun in Bukavu one day, they mentioned the two needs. "I've been looking for someone to come here," she said. Then she took them to a beautiful place in the city with five bedrooms, two bathrooms, family dining room, office and fireplace.

"But you don't understand," Sam Vinton said to Mme. DeKun, "We can't afford that. We are missionaries."

Undaunted, she replied, "If God led you here, maybe He wants you to have a nice place to stay."

After finding the owner and negotiating terms, Mme. DeKun came to Baba Vi again.

"Here's your house," she said. "Pay for it when you can. Just sign these papers and it's yours."

Similarly, the Lord gave the Vintons the best bookshop in town as their literature center, with free use for the first three years—after which they rented the property.

When the rebels' scorched-earth policy destroyed all the mission trucks, God again provided in various ways. Oxfam sent out a Landrover. UN sent out a truck, and the Zaire Protestant Relief Agency sent two trucks. Because they were for medical work, no duty was required.

After the rebellion had ended, Sam Vinton Sr. received a letter from 37 village chiefs.

"Baba Vi," it read, "we want you back. All we have to offer is our hands. We are willing to do anything to rebuild Kama station if you will come back."

With that letter in hand, the veteran missionary went to the United Nations authorities. Among other things, he obtained one-and-a-half tons of salt. (The people had gone ten months without salt in their food; ten *days* without salt in America would be calamitous!)

In 1964, Sam and Marie Vinton superintended the building of the Kama airstrip—"the only airstrip in all the country that cost no money to build." Laborers received used clothing as pay. Missionary Wayne Schoonover engineered the entire landing strip, working long hours in leveling and hauling gravel.

"Marie had as many as 500 women and children working on the airstrip," Baba Vi said. "At other times, a hundred men labored on the strip. After a full year of work, the 2500-foot dirt airstrip—the Kama lifeline—was completed." Three pilots who evacuated missionaries during the rebellion called it the best airstrip in the area.

Tales of individual heroism during the uprisings were common. When the Vintons and other missionaries were held as prisoners in Kindu, the nationals were forbidden to approach white men.

"I have come to see Baba Vi," Abraham Bulahimu said to one of the guards. "If you want to shoot me, go ahead, but I'm going to see him." His persistence paid off.

Many years later, during the 45th anniversary celebration at Luyamba, beaming, grey-haired Abraham greeted Baba Vi and Henry Sonneveldt warmly. They recalled the earlier days of turmoil and trial, made bearable by good fellowship.

Only once, in 1961, did the rebels actually inflict physical harm to the Vintons. This came about when Baba Vi refused to make a mockery of prayer by asking for God's blessing on all that was taking place in the rebellion. Hit on the elbow with the butt of a gun, Sam rolled over and was severely injured.

When one of the rebel officers saw what had happened to Vinton, he turned on the attacker furiously. "If anything happens to this missionary before we get to Kindu, I'll kill you," he said.

That typified many instances in which God used the wrath of man to praise Him—by protecting His servants. Knowing how Vinton would react to violence, even in retaliation, the officer said to Baba Vi, "Let me handle this. It isn't religion any more; it's military!"

Vinton observed, "We didn't lose one missionary during all of the uprisings." In 1964, he gave a firsthand report of the dramatic Battle of Bukavu:

"These past days and nights have been something we'll never forget. We have felt the prayers of the saints—thank them for us. At this writing, we are in Shangugu, (now Cyangugu) Rwanda, at the Swedish Mission on the hill just above the Kamembe airport where Sonneveldt and the Hammonds flew into when they came to Bukavu in April.

"We see the planes coming and going, all day long, mostly the fighter planes. But since the Battle of Bukavu started, the C-130 U.S. transports have been arriving at least every day."

Baba Vi continued: "The day the battle broke, we were all at the

Bukavu guest house—Helen Gow of the Berean Mission, Helen Hoffman and Dorothy Rudge of the ESAM, and Marie and I. The U.S. Consul called us at 2:30 p.m. and told us to get out in a hurry. We did—and are thankful for it.

"Now that the rebels were driven out, we went over to Bukavu today to hold a service with the Christians there, and it was a real time of rejoicing. They all had wonderful stories to tell of how God miraculously took care of them through the raging battles in the city.

"All the mission buildings are safe in Bukavu. Our guest house is as we left it: perfect. The literature center had six window panes broken. There were 16 bullet holes in the glass panes. But God had protected all the believers."

Vinton added: "The Theological Center had only one pane of glass broken. These are all miracles. God put a wall around our property—I should say *His* property.

"We had rooms in the hotel in Shangugu, but gave them up on the day of the battle to others—women and children—and we have been sleeping in our car out on the hill overlooking the airport and the city of Bukavu.

"In daylight we could look right down at the guest house about a mile and a half away. We could follow the battle and street fighting—especially at night; also the planes as they went out to shoot rockets at rebel reinforcements."

Concluding his report, Baba Vi added: "We are leaving August 24 by plane for Usumbura to have a time of counsel with Sam Jr. and Becky. We shall return to Bukavu the next day. Tell the saints to rejoice with us, and to keep praying."

Early in 1965, Vinton reported "We had the little plane bring out Pastors Albert Mukula, Yakobo Bitingo and Stanislas Twambe—and we've been listening ever since.

"Our hearts overflow with joy and praise as we hear that all of our pastors on the Kama-Pangi road are safe and alive. This is wonderful, and we do praise the Lord.

"We have no word of our pastors on the Kampene road through the Mwanga. However, the same God who took care of the Pangi field is also taking care of the Kampene area."

But not all the nationals escaped the treachery of war and rebellion. "Chief Andre Kibonge was beheaded," Vinton added, "as was Kitingi, whom Chris and Edna Mae Egemeier led to the Lord. He was a real man of God. Both these chiefs were men of special value, and their going is a great loss to our Beia field. We must pray that the right men will be raised up to take over.

"Some 46 villages have been burned to the ground and more than 2,500 families in the Kama area are homeless—and all their earthly possessions are lost.

"Add to this the 1,200 homeless families in the Itula-Zingu-Kalole field and you can see that we are faced with a major disaster. This is a tremendous challenge and an overwhelming responsibility. Among those almost 4,000 homeless families are perhaps 1,500 believers."

Sam Vinton was not one to paint glowing pictures of drama and adventure to potential missionaries. Describing the situation further at that time, he said:

"Our great need is personnel. We must plan on sending teams of two missionaries at a time into the bush. There will be danger for several years of bandits jumping out and taking your car at the point of a gun. It may even be necessary to enter with a military escort."

By late July of 1965, Vinton had a more encouraging report:

"Ernie Green and I are just back from our trip to the burned-out areas—my third. We spent a night and a day at Kama, where we received a tremendous reception.

"All the brick buildings are intact and are being occupied by the Congolese army. The Kama population is returning and work is beginning, praise God."

Vinton added: "We took Amici Musa, one of our own medical boys, with us and set him up. The rebel captives are now cleaning up the medical center, which is the only one in a radius of 100 miles with personnel and supplies.

"The lepers are returning. We gave them salt—the first they have had in nearly a year. How good it is to be able to help them.

"At least 100 families of the mission population are back and must start from scratch. But all are beaming and enthusiastic about rebuilding Kama, now that they know we are with them."

Baba Vi then described some of the help he received from various agencies.

"The UN sent $1,500 in food with which to pay nationals to put Kama medical center back into shape. The chief and the people are working on the airstrip. The army is making a new ferry out of the old one.

"The Congo Protestant Relief Agency is shipping food, clothing, blankets and school supplies from Leopoldville to Kindu by river and rail; also more from New York through Dar es Salaam. And praise God for 28 barrels of clothing, goods and tools just received from home."

After receiving 2,000 machetes through Bujumbura, Vinton observed:

"What a big thing they are in the lives of these people. We gave Bibles to all the pastors and New Testaments to all the church elders. Now all the chiefs want Bibles, too. A full ton of literature came last week from the Bible Societies in London and New York.

"We cannot go through a village anywhere along the roads

112

without hearing cries for literature. So we must keep supplies coming in and have a different tract for each trip."

Vinton concluded: "The home study Bible courses are in high gear in the Beia area where Albert Mukula set up a bureau. Nearly 1,000 are enrolled already. Pastor Andre Asumani took 1,000 with him to Kama on this last trip."

By the end of the year, Baba Vi reported that an estimated 6,000 families in the Kama area alone are homeless, having lost all their earthly possessions. Medical care, clothing, vitamins, milk for babies and children, comprise the immediate needs. These items should be made available as quickly as possible.

When 80 tons of food arrived in Kindu from the United States, Vinton explained his dilemma:

"It is wonderful to have all this food, but we are now faced with a tremendous problem of transporting it to the Kama area. There is no public transport in Kindu. The mines are handicapped by lack of trucks for their own work, so we are in desperate need."

Thanks to intervention by the American vice-consul in Bukavu, US/AID stepped in to ease the situation, helping with the needed hauling and distribution of food.

By late 1966, Vinton was able to report: "The city of Bukavu is quite normal and all our activities are being carried on in full swing, for which we do praise the Lord.

"Our bookshop sales the third quarter of the year reached a total of almost $1,600. More than 36,000 items were sold each month. Pray that the Word of the Lord may have free course and be glorified.

"Things have opened up in Kama so that it is now feasible for missionary couples without children to take up residence. However, due to the widespread looting which took place, the missionary homes will have to be refurnished."

Regarding the Mwanga station, Baba Vi reported: "Missionaries have not visited this place since the rebels took over in 1964. The area has been liberated, however, and church leaders are busy getting church and school activities under way.

"The Wazimba people in the area are anxious to have missionaries, and are pressing for the construction of an airstrip near the Mwanga station. This will be a community development project.

"There is a real need for a literature distribution and evangelistic center in Kasongo. Pastor Bulahimu has indicated his willingness to return to Kasongo and take up the ministry he was performing there several years ago."

Regarding Kayembe, Vinton reported: "Church leaders here have made several overtures to the Mission, requesting to be reinstated. Fellowship was broken some years ago when certain leaders on this station seized Mission property and sold it for their own gain."

Early in 1967, Baba Vi said: "The Kama dispensary has been repaired and is functioning to the extent that the limited supplies of medicines permit. Pre-natal clinics are being conducted, and the maternity center has resumed activities under the direction of two well-trained Congolese midwives.

"Distribution of used clothing, medical samples, vitamins and seeds continues as the Lord supplies.

"Most important of all, the Kama church continues to function along with branch churches in many surrounding villages. The Gospel of the grace of God is being preached. Individuals are committing themselves to Christ.

"The Bible Institute is once again preparing young men for the ministry. The primary schools conducted by the Mission are taught by Christian teachers who are concerned not only with secular instruction, but also with systematic Bible teaching."

Much more could be said about rebellions and uprisings in Zaire, but the primary purpose here is not to chronicle the history of war but rather to honor God for His faithfulness through trial and tribulation in the lives of Sam and Marie Vinton and their colleagues.

In the face of all that has gone on, and the present and future potential, have these missionaries any special words of wisdom for young people today who might be contemplating a lifetime of service for the Lord?

CHAPTER 15

Leave Your Footprints

When Dan Bultema returned from a 1976 trip to the field, again accompanied by Henry Sonneveldt, he listed several objectives, priorities and goals for the Zaire ministries.

"The further development of Theological Education by Extension (TEE) will have high priority.

"Another priority item is to provide higher theological education for some of our most capable young African leaders. This would mean sending them to a good conservative theological school at Bunia.

"This is vital if we are to raise the level of their effectiveness in imparting the Word of God.

"There must be an increasing emphasis on the production and distribution of Swahili literature. There is a desperate cry for something to read throughout the Kivu region, and it is tragic that there is so little to read.

"Our Zaire pastors need study books and the Christians need good devotional reading. Though we have shipped tons of Swahili literature, we have only scratched the surface.

"The best literature, of course, is the Word of God. For the past few years, it has been practically impossible to obtain Swahili Bibles or New Testaments.

"Three months ago, Sam Vinton finally was able to get 8,000 New Testaments at two dollars each. While we were in Zaire, we were overjoyed to learn that we could get 10,000 Swahili New Testaments specially printed by the London Bible Society for only one dollar each.

"Sam jumped for joy when we told him that some $10,000 has been received from Christians in America enabling us to place an order while we were in Nairobi for 10,000 New Testaments with a promise of delivery within six months."

Bultema suggested one final goal for Zaire. "We want to develop additional airstrips for our area. Automotive transportation is becoming almost impossible. Many bridges are out and the cost of gasoline is almost prohibitive. So air transportation is a must, and additional airstrips must have high priority."

Sonneveldt added: "If we are to meet the challenge of church growth, it is imperative that qualified missionary candidates step out in faith to volunteer for this ministry."

Years ago, Sam Vinton told an audience of young people, "Wherever you go to serve the Lord, be sure to leave your footprints."

Today, the veteran missionary has some additional thoughts for young men and women:

"I am overwhelmed" he says, "working harder right now — at 72 — than I have ever worked before during my career in Africa. Why? Because the demands from the people are still here.

"As soon as we get out of our living room, we are confronted with people who want our help. We need young people to come out and help us take care of this load."

Mr. Vinton then suggests a second reason for considering Kama as a place of service for the Lord.

"I don't believe there is any area in the world where the door is open any wider or where the people are more eager and responsive than here in the Kama area.

"This is the very time that the area should be saturated with the gospel of Christ Jesus. If the people are hungry, and they are, God will speak to them through His Word."

In the third place, Baba Vi continues, "I definitely believe that God has planned that we reach these people now. *This is the time.*

"Have we failed to present the need? Are young people too busy to hear God's voice? Are there so many interruptions in the work, so many rebellions and uprisings, that they are fearful of coming out?

"God is not going to let people be hungry just to tantalize them. If God has planted hunger in the hearts of these people, He expects someone to feed them. This is the time of reaping.

"If you have a desire to share Christ, to teach the Word of God, to do agricultural work, to engage in educational, manual labor or carpentry programs, *COME TO KAMA.*"

One thing remains crystal clear: Young people must begin to respond quickly if the significant, exciting ministry begun by Sam and Marie Vinton many years ago is to continue and flourish.

DATE DUE